The Calico Golem

DARIAN HART

The Calico Golem
Darian Hart

© 2024 Oxford eBooks Ltd.

Published under the sci-fi-cafe.com imprint.
www.oxford-ebooks.com

The right of the author to be identified as the author of this work
has been asserted in accordance with the
Copyright, Designs and Patents Act 1988.

Illustrations and cover art by Catrina Parton

ISBN 978-1-910779-14-9 (Paperback)

sci-fi-cafe.com

Also by Darian Hart

The Wolf Inside Us

CHAPTER 1

EMILY HAD LAID her microwave Christmas dinner for one out onto a plate in an attempt to make it at least *look* like a proper meal. Two meagre slices of turkey glistened with suspicious looking gravy in the light of the TV.

It was almost 3pm and what grey and depressing light the day had to offer was already fading.

"Hey, fancy-pants." Mads joined her on the couch and plopped her plastic plate on the coffee table. Somehow, the small black disc, warped with the heat conspired looked more full than Emily's.

She grinned back, cracked open a can of cider and carefully filled their one and only wine glass. "Merry Christmas!" She offered the glass to toast. Mads obliged with a sigh and clunked her can against the overfilled glass. A little spilled over the edge and Emily set to licking her fingers.

The TV faded to an image of Buckingham Palace. Emily reached for the remote and turned up the sound.

"Can't miss this," she said through a mouthful of rubbery roast potato, "The Kings *first* speech."

"I'd never've taken you for a royalist." Mads stabbed at a yellowish sprout end eyed it with contempt.

"I wouldn't say that. I mean the Queen was lovely, you can't argue that can you?"

Mads nodded agreement and opened her drink. It spurted and she quickly put it to her mouth to catch the foam. She opened her eyes to a McDonalds paper napkin dangling in front of her face. She gulped and mopped the can, then the table.

"It's a little bit of history," Emily continued, picking another napkin from the pile on her side of the table and handing it over.

Mads rolled her eyes and ran a finger through Emily's long, black hair. She turned and smiled, eyes black as her hair glittered back in the reflected light of the new monarch.

"How do you always stay so positive?" Her tone began almost in wonder, but her face began to sag. She looked around the dimly lit room with its ancient, mismatched furniture. The curtains were open to the dirty grey light of the city. Other tower blocks loomed nearby, dark and menacing – the same rotting concrete as their own, lifting them up from the filthy and dangerous streets below.

She put her fork down onto the plastic and looked

again into those eyes that held her spellbound every time she saw them. Moisture began to line the bottom lids of her own eyes, a stark contrast to those of her lover. Powder blue, edged with green, her lashes, thick and white, like explosions.

"I mean," she gestured to the walls, "we've been here... what, three years now and what do we have to show for it? Is this the best we can do for ourselves?" Frustration built, and for a moment she wanted to slap the pathetic meal onto the floor, but she knew that they simply couldn't afford to waste food. "Even if we could afford a proper turkey with all the trimmings, we don't even have an oven... or the money to run the bloody thing." The tears were starting to flow now.

Emily sat, silent and patient. She had nothing to offer except her attention.

"I know you work hard to make the best of things." She felt a little bad about her reference to the flat, "God knows you keep this little place gleaming, and I honestly don't know how you make the crap that I earn last."

"I'll try again for a job in the new year," Emily said softly, "That new Aldi looks like it's almost finished. They'll be hiring now, I'm sure."

"I know you try." Mads sighed and took Emily's hand in hers. She looked at her thin, delicate fingers in her own huge hands. "I should really try to do a little more around the house... but I just get so tired with things."

Emily squeezed her fingers, "Perhaps, the shower? The drain's blocked."

"Again?" Mads scoffed, choking back a laugh

that threatened to bring more tears with it, "I had to wrestle the bride of Cthulu out of there just last week." She ran her hand through her own, clipped white afro, "You can bet that it's not me. And down there," she chuckled, pointing to Emily's lap. Emily looked down, letting her glossy hair fall over her face like a black waterfall. "I feel like Doctor Livingstone on date nights!"

Emily looked up impishly, peering through her hair with a grin.

"Shit, girl. I sometimes wonder if I need a guide with me." She stopped. Emily was looking back at her, silent as a ghost in the dimly lit room, pale white face half illuminated by the TV, her eyes just sparks of reflected light. God, she was so sweet... creepy, but sweet.

"Look, I'm sorry," Mads began, "I didn't mean to make fun. I love your hair – all of it. I mean, look think what we save on dental floss."

"Ew! Mads, really?" She punched her arm and returned to her food, smirking to herself in the gloom.

Darkness had now fully engulfed the little flat. The only light in the room, save for the tiny string of LED Christmas lights adorning a sickly cactus in the corner was the TV.

The girls lay together on the couch, as much for warmth as for comfort. Emily felt at ease wrapped in Mads' muscular arms, the gentle rhythm of her breathing a constant reassurance.

The volume of the TV wasn't especially high, and across the sound of the show – Emily wasn't really paying much attention, the sounds of life around them drifted in from the street below, the walls, the ceiling. Occasional drags of a chair from above, a slammed door from the teenager living next to them, a shout from the street then a laugh. All sounds of people living their lives, better lives then her, she hoped.

A bright flash of light and a plaintive grumble announced a message on Mads' phone. She grunted and leaned across to grab it from the coffee table, slightly crushing Emily in the process and advancing the battle between laying in comfort and needing to get up for a pee.

"Sorry," Mads muttered, pulling herself up to sit; the screen blasted her face with light that made Emily squint and look away. Purple-blue rectangles danced in her vision as she tried to blink them away.

"What is it?" she asked sitting up carefully now realising how full her bladder really was.

"Ugh. Work stuff. Can you believe it?"

"Today? What?"

"Looks like there's been a mix up with the shifts. Mike wants me to work tomorrow, needs to talk with a bunch of us..." She paused, reading the rest of the message, "Supermarket's closed of course so we're meeting at the Greyhound... For fu– In half an hour. Oh," she feigned delight, "Mike's buying the drinks."

Emily sagged, "They can't DO that. Not on Christmas Day. Don't go."

"Double time, Chick. God knows we need the money. And I'm gonna get a drink out of that tight fucker if it kills me."

"He's a bloody screw-up." Emily rarely got angry,

but her fists were balled up now. "He had one job to do, sort out the shifts. How hard can that be, what's wrong wi– bollocks, I've got to pee." She hurried off into the darkness, light spilling briefly into to the hallway before the bathroom door slammed shut.

Mads unfolded from the couch. It was saggy and old, but hell it was comfortable. She stretched and padded over to the window. Below, in the street two cars were parked side by side, the drivers chatting through rolled-down windows. A billow of vape erupted from one car and slowly drifted away into the cold night air.

She pulled the curtains closed and turned on the small lamp in the corner of the room.

Behind her, the sound of the toilet flushing and the pop-click of the pull cord. Emily emerged out of the darkness, like a Japanese ghost – all scowls and waist-long hair.

"Go, if you have to," she muttered. "But why choose *that place?* It's a dump."

"You think Mike's got class?" She shrugged and grabbed her trainers from next to the door and crouched to lace them up.

"I'll be back as soon as I can, chicken." She smiled, planting a kiss on her forehead.

"Don't call me chicken," she moped, but threw her arms around her and hugged her tightly, looking for all the world like a child.

"Can't help it," she beamed, "It's that cute little pecker of yours."

With that, she turned and left, humming gently to herself.

CHAPTER 2

MADELINE'S CHEEKY PARTING remark left a little smile on Emily's face for a full ten minutes. After that, the sense of being by herself began to seep into her like cold, damp air.

In an attempt to save money, they often left most of the lights off. Frustratingly, this Christmas there was no Doctor Who special, so she had switched off the TV in disgust. The only useful light in the living room now was the orange glow from the street lights below and the light pollution from the blanket of miserable clouds overhead.

She wandered over to the window and stared at the block opposite. Little squares of colour – other people's lives stretched out above and below her.

She pulled herself away from the window before she started to wonder what those lives must be like and then inevitably compare them to her own.

With nothing much else to do, Emily made her way across the living room in the gloom to the bedroom and flopped down onto the bed. She let out her breath in a long expression of boredom.

She sat up with a little squeak of delight, remembering the gift that Mads had bought her. She turned over and switched on the bedside lamp, reaching for the book. It was a large, thick hardback – the coffee table type. She looked at the cover, glossy dark with the snarling figure of a zombie reaching out its bony hand.

There was just one tiny scuff in the corner of the spine. Mads had apologised that she had to buy it on eBay, the original was way too expensive. That didn't matter one bit, Emily was a devoted fan of Jake Mayer, and just to own the official memorial art book was enough. She loved it.

Pulling herself into a sitting position, she opened the book in her lap and flipped through the thick, glossy pages. She stopped briefly on a bright assault of colour where the book talked about his other creations, the obscenely popular *Princess Sparkles* franchise. These multi-coloured unicorns had made him a millionaire almost overnight.

How the hell, she wondered had someone so young become so successful? But of course everything has its price. She had read the story she knew so well in the book about his crippling agoraphobia and tragic death.

A tear formed in the corner of her eye. Wiping it away with the sleeve of her jumper, she wondered who it was for. Was it for the tragic artist she so admired, was it that she felt a connection? He, herself, mads, all freaks in a way, outcasts, strange.

How long would Mads be? She'd only been gone half an hour but she felt so alone, she wanted Mads here, she needed to be held tightly in her strong arms, feel her warm, soft body against hers keeping her safe.

Under the lamp to her right sat the little fabric doll that Mads had made for her years ago. She put the heavy book to one side and picked up the little figure, squeezed it, felt the rustle of beans inside it, held it close to her chest.

Smiling serenely now, she lay back and looked into the tiny black bead-like eyes. If she turned it just right in the lamp light, she could just about make out her reflection. This little thing always reminded her so much of Mads whenever she was gone. But it also held some of the most painful memories of her young life.

Emily closed her eyes holding the doll close to her and slowly drifted away to sleep.

There was a small area of dense woodland, accessible through a broken chain-link fence at the far end of the school playing field. This was the secret spot which anyone up to no good assumed that nobody else knew about.

A littering of cigarette butts, disposable vapes and little metal bottles was a testament to that.

Within the wood, off the beaten path, Mads pushed aside the fleshy leaves of a giant rhododendron bush to reveal the hollow interior. Multiple trunks as thick as Mads' arm twisted, spiralled and split from the centre of the space. Branches had been carefully snapped off by years of previous clandestines to create a perfect shelter, away from prying eyes.

Emily stooped and stepped inside, mouth open in awe. "It's wonderful," she breathed in quiet reverence like this was some chapel or sacred space.

"We'll be fine here," Mads was almost on her knees entering the hollow. "But keep it quiet, there might be others later back by the fence."

Emily dropped her bag, heavy with revision books – her GCSEs were coming up in a couple of weeks and her life was almost completely absorbed by revision. The chance to break away from all that, even for a moment. was a delight.

She sat against a gnarled trunk, legs stretched out on the dry leaves on the forest floor and let out a contented sigh. The light was dim, and green and cool in here a delicious respite from the hot summer's afternoon.

She looked up to the canopy of leaves above and caught glimpses of a nearby oak – they were wrapped in layers of green, away from everyone and everything.

Mads knelt down beside Emily – Emily opened her mouth to speak but Mads raised a hand, she looked up and drank in the silence and the peace of the place. Emily understood, and closed her mouth.

Mads leaned a little closer, looking deeply into the

dark depths of Emily's eyes, her hair hung down behind her head and over her shoulders.

Emily returned the gaze, her eyes tracing around the edges of the port-wine birthmark on her face, under her left ear, round her strong jawline to the corner of her full, lips made proud by her Jamacan ancestry. The coastline of her birthmark ran along the side of her nose to circle her eye and lose itself under the white, short fuzz of her hair.

For days, Emily had been transfixed by the sight of her, had wanted to just stare with abandon, swim in every detail of her face and her body. The mark on her face no longer a startling disfigurement, but the shores of some far away and exotic island, drawn on the white albino skin of the most remarkable person she had ever seen.

For Madelene, it was the same. She was used to being different, and so felt that everyone else was plain, uninteresting, not worthy of a second look. Emily was different; they were kin and they both revelled in it.

Nervously, Emily leaned a little closer, pulling her knees up a little off the soft, dry leaves. Mads blinked slowly and gently shook her head. *Not yet.*

She reached out and placed the palm of her hand on Emily's belly, just below the navel and held it there, feeling the slow movement of her breathing.

Emily sighed and parted her legs a little. The warmth of Mads' hand on her flowed out from her like warm honey.

Her groin flushed with heat, aching for attention, and with it her deepest and most deadly secret began to stir, engorging and pressing against her underwear – nothing to rival any of the boys in her class, but becoming obvious nonetheless as she edged her knees further apart.

She gazed into Mads' green eyes, imploring, and shifted her buttocks leaning back into the tree.

Mads had seen her like this a couple of weeks ago; just one glimpse and instantly she had been fascinated.

The long, hot summer was just beginning and she had been training on the track in the last period of the day. She ought to have been revising for her A-Levels but running was the only thing which truly took away her stress.

The last P.E. class had finished -- fifteen more minutes on the track at maximum effort left her gasping but at peace. The changing rooms ought to be free by now she estimated so headed back into the main school building.

As she reached out to push open the changing room door it burst open and three girls stopped dead, looking up at Mads in the doorway. They were silent for a beat then pushed under her arm erupting into giggles down the corridor.

The changing room seemed empty, save for some trash and a discarded towel on the floor. Mads picked it up and dropped it onto a bench before slipping out of her shorts and shirt. She scowled at a large grass stain on the back where she had tripped earlier and dumped her underwear on top of the pile.

Still slick with sweat, she padded into the showers to cool off from the baking summer heat.

She heard the sound of water running before she got there; one small girl was still showering, standing silently in the thin trickle of warm water. Her back to the other girl, she paid no heed and stepped under the water to let it soak her.

A slight unease crept over her as she wiped the suds from her face. The girl had turned to face her and was watching her shower, silently gazing at her stocky, athletic physique – long cascades of black hair plastered to her shoulders and all but covered the girl's breasts.

Mads smiled uneasily and glanced down at the enormous mass of black hair between her legs, and at the little pink protrusion nestling there.

It twitched.

The girl seemed to snap from a trance, then covering herself fled silently from the showers.

Mads quickly washed the soap from her face and followed the girl to the changing room to find her hastily towelling herself off and pulling her clothes together.

Mads stepped towards her, still naked "Are you alright?" she asked.

The girl held the towel tightly and glanced up at Mads, standing boldly, unashamed.

"Sorry," she mumbled, then began again, "Sorry, it doesn't usually do that by itself," the girl blushed.

"Just when you're thinking about some hot boy?" Mads smirked cheerfully, "You seemed to be having a daydream just now."

"Um, no, I don't really think about boys..." she hesitated again, stealing a glance at Madeline's muscular thighs, "Not in that way."

"Ah. Me too." Mads picks up her towel and begins drying herself. "Yeah, I've had the odd crush on a couple of girls before, but they're all so... boring." She stopped and smiled at the strange girl, "You're different. Cute."

Embarrassed, Emily began fumbling for her clothes, quickly pulled on her pants which of course put up a struggle against her still-damp skin. She began to untangle the skirt she'd dumped on the bench, "I've seen you out running a few times. You're kind of unique yourself," she muttered, pulling on her skirt.

"Ha, yes. Scares most people off. But I'm used to it."

"It's hard being different," said Emily, sadly. She looked up from fiddling with a stuck zip to see Mads was already in a clean pair of shorts and was hitching up her bra.

"I think I've come to embrace it. My body's different, so I may as well make something of it." She flexed her muscular physique briefly, grinning broadly.

Emily smiled and lowered her gaze demurely.

"I used to think that is was normal," Mads continued, "I'd always kept to myself, maybe I was a bit slow to catch on to noticing boys perhaps. And the other girls—"

"—Nobody wants to be your friend when you're different." Emily cut in, seeming to gain a little confidence. She swept the hair from her face and looked up to Mads.

Pulling on a white t-shirt with a black stylised skull on the front, Mads took a leap of faith, "Look, don't think I'm hitting on you or anything but do you want to go grab a coffee or something after? There's a place on the high street that makes a brilliant cherry pie."

Emily hesitated for a moment and seemed to come to a decision. "Okay, why not. My parents wont be back from work for a couple of hours, I won't be missed."

Under the canopy, out of the still-hot afternoon sun, the air was perfectly warm.

With a tiny whimper, Emily lifted her skirt and pushed her pants aside to allow her little curiosity to stand free in the open air, inviting attention, filling the space with her sweet, warm aroma. Her pale face now beginning to flush, she looked to Mads again, her eyes pleading.

Appearing to relent, the older girl shifted, but kept a firm pressure on Emily's stomach. Her free hand, she slid slowly down into her own shorts, not breaking eye contact for a microsecond. The silence in their perfect shelter was absolute, any other noise, or rustle of leaves in the breeze had stopped.

Mads withdrew her hand gently with the most delicate of sounds, as if she had opened her mouth to whisper a secret... and pressed two fingers to Emily's lips as if to hush her.

The narcotic aroma of her musk flooded Emily's senses until she felt that she would certainly lose all sense of self and even consciousness.

How do you do it? How can you hold back Mads? I can't take it any more, I—

"Fucking Hell, a pair of lezzers!" A boy's voice

shattered the air, like splinters of granite. "Lads, quick!"

Mads span and toppled to her back as the gurning teen thrust his head inside their sanctuary, gawping at Emily, prone, exposed, frozen with fear.

"Fuck me, she's got a nob!" the boy yelled. The others could be heard scrambling through the woods. A growl began to build in Mads' throat – and then it happened. The final dagger of humiliation was thrust into Emily's heart the instant an uncontrollable spray of pee burst out from between her legs, spattering noisily onto the dry leaves.

"Get the FUCK out!" Mads screamed, finally finding her voice.

Emily pulled her knees together and dragged herself into a crouch, sobbing while rivulets of pee ran down her thighs hot as shame, washing dirt and bits of leaf down and into her shoes and socks.

A second head appeared, behind the screen of his phone.

Quick as lightning, the boy grabbed Emily's bag from the floor but as he made his retreat Mads burst from the ground. At that same instant a tornado exploded inside the hollow bush, leaves, sticks, a mist of urine all whirled around as Mads flew at Ian.

Her weighty fist caught him just above the eye sending him staggering backwards into the next of the boys to arrive. The back of his head burst his nose messily.

The two boys fled, yelling for the others to get away from the crazy freak in the woods.

Mads took off after them, but they were small,

weedy little weasels and dove through the broken fence like it wasn't there and away into the playing field, whooping and yelling.

Mads stopped at the fence as they turned and jeered at a safe distance.

The first boy threw Emily's bag over to his friend, he caught it deftly and swung it over his head, then pulled it open. The contents of Emily's bag were tossed into the air as they cackled.

The first boy, she recognised him now, Ian Thompson, yanked Emily's cloth cat from the string on her empty bag. He looked back at Mads, blood streaming from the cut over his eye, dropped the bag and raised the toy in his trembling fist.

"You're both fucked!" he yelled, and tore the little cat to pieces before marching away.

Mads stood for a long moment, trying to process what had just happened – how what would have been a perfect, special moment with this sweet, utterly enchanting girl had disintegrated into misery. *Emily. Shit, she was all alone.*

"Em! Em, I'm so sorr—" She burst into the bush den to find it empty.

The bullies were long gone when Mads reached the place where they had thrown Emily's belongings. She picked everything up and carefully put them back into her rucksack. Amongst the strewn books, pencil case and assorted bits, a graphic novel which she recognised fluttered lazily in the languid breeze. She smiled to herself as she slid it safely inside the bag and turned to the remains of her little cloth cat.

It was an old thing, baggy, somewhat loose at the

seams which had made it all the easier for Ian to tear it apart, but Mads knew that Emily loved it.

Some of the stuffing had blown away, but after scouring the area she thought that she had all the bits. It was utterly ruined, she knew. She stood for a moment in thought, then a little smile crept across her face.

She was ready to break down when she arrived, breathless at the door, then realising that her keys were in her stolen bag she scrambled at the pile of cobbles in the back garden, tears and snot running down her face until she found the hidden key.

With a crash, the front door burst open and slammed shut. Emily thundered up the stairs in sobs that threatened to take the very breath from her body.

Emily turned the shower on full blast, tearing at her dirty and stinking clothes as steam began to fill the bathroom.

She squirted a huge palmful of shower gel into her hands and frantically scrubbed the bits of leaf and mud from her hair, her legs, even her most intimate areas were host to the dirt that had whipped around in a sudden and inexplicable tornado inside their leafy sanctuary.

Calming a little, her mind drifted back to the events of the afternoon, heart racing again then angry at the interruption.

Frantically, she finished what she had so desperately wanted Mads to start; then as the remainder of the soap ran down her thighs the tears began to flow again.

Until now, she had just followed what seemed natural – being with Mads was the happiest she had ever felt, but she hadn't given the whole thing any real thought.

But now, it had a name – crudely announced by the bullies – but there it was, the truth. She *was* gay. This was her life now, this was who, what she truly was.

CHAPTER 3

WHATEVER IT WAS that woke Emily from her sleep she wasn't sure. At first, she thought she had heard Mads coming back home, but it must have been some other sound – maybe from the next flat, or somebody outside on the walkway. Her initial excitement gave way to the echoes of the dream, fading like rolling thunder. It left her with an empty feeling of sadness and anger.

She scratched at an itch on her cheek to find it soaked with tears. Her other hand still tightly clutched at the little fabric doll.

The lock-screen on her phone informed her with cold indifference that it was half past nine. She had slept for *hours*, and yet Mads was not back. Being all alone was one thing, she didn't really mind that – besides, solitude is different to loneliness – but on Christmas Day?

This was just too much.

By the light of the little bedroom lamp, she pulled herself off the bed, rubbed her eyes and ventured into the living room. It was dark and silent.

Outside on the walkway, a neighbour was leaning over the concrete wall smoking a cigarette. He puffed a cloud of smoke out into the void as Emily closed the door behind her and carefully locked it.

He grinned and nodded towards her, she stuffed the key into a zippered pocket of her black leather jacket, smiled weakly back to him and hurried past towards the stairwell.

The lifts, of course hadn't worked in all the time she had lived here but at least *most* of the lights down the six stories of concrete stairs worked.

The rubbish and acrid urine stench didn't make an appearance until the final two flights of steps; she increased her pace to get past it as quickly as she could while trying not to breathe too deeply. The fabric doll flapped against her thigh, suspended by a chain from the wide black belt atop a thick blue and yellow tartan skirt.

Rounding the last landing, she carefully avoided touching the filthy handrails and stepped out into the concrete parking area between her block and the identical one opposite.

A gust of icy midwinter air greeted her like a waiting dog, though the only things it dropped to her shin-high boots were a couple of empty crisp packets. A ragged mass of chip-paper ambled greasily past, like tumbleweed in a cheesy western movie.

Another frigid blast had Emily wishing she'd chosen her heavy black dress instead of the black and grey striped stockings she had on. Because she was going to that nasty dive of a pub, she'd opted for something a little more mainstream to wear over her usual 'gothic but not necessarily Goth' look. Besides, if things kicked off, it would be hard to run swathed in heavy black velvet.

With her jacket pulled tightly to her petite body against the winter night, she forged ahead. Trotting quickly down the steps to the underpass, she found a young man sitting in the flickering neon.

As she entered the tunnel, he looked up at her from within his grubby hoodie and brought a thumb-sized glass vial to his mouth. With a faint hiss, a glowing purple vapour wafted out. The junkie quickly inhaled the cloudlet of gas and allowed a little snort of laughter to escape.

Emily shook her head and picked up her pace even though she knew that this guy wouldn't be bothering her at all now. She glanced back over her shoulder to find him rocking back and forth humming a nursery rhyme to himself, grinning stupidly.

The Pub – *The Greyhound* – wasn't what a lot of people would really call a pub. It probably used to be a working man's social club in the 70's and didn't really look like it had seen a lick of paint since then either. The entrance to the car park had been blocked with a couple of large concrete rings filled with soil, topped with trash and the skeletal remains of some kind of plant. They were probably there to deter doggers and druggies, Emily thought.

Despite the smoking ban in pubs way back in '07, the stench of stale cigarettes and spilled beer assaulted Emily's nostrils as she pushed the half-glazed door open.

It lazily eased itself closed behind her on a gummed up sprung hinge.

The door had hardly closed when a rowdy cheer came from a small group at the bar.

"Oi oi, here she is!" Was the prelude to an eruption of jeers and cackles. It was *them*, the gang of boys that had made her life hell in school. Her blood ran cold, not so much with fear as anger – icy hatred.

The guys leaning at the bar turned to watch Emily walk over to the corner where Mads was gathered with several others. She rose from her seat and drew Emily into a warm hug, the smell of cider strong on her.

The idiots at the bar seemed to enjoy that, one knocking his glass over with a crash prompting renewed cheering.

"Just ignore them," Mads whispered, glaring over Emily's shoulder at Ian. "They were losers at school, and they still are."

"Are you nearly done?" she asked quietly.

"Yeah, looks like I'm off the hook until the twenty-eighth."

"That's good," Emily smiled and kissed her chin, "Got you all to myself for a couple of days." She smiled cheekily. Then felt Mads stiffen and growl.

"Oi, Lezzers. Go get a room or summink."

The chatter at the table behind them stopped.

"Shove off Ian." Emily snarled with more bravado than she really felt.

"What? You gonna make me?" he jeered, waving a nearly full pint of lager unsteadily.

It had been at least three years since Emily had seen Ian and his cronies. She had assumed that they had moved on, but like her and Mads, they were still living in the same town that they grew up in. Images of the hell that they had put her through, the pain, the ultimate *cost* to her tumbled around in her mind. The incident in the sanctuary washed to the forefront.

With an odd little splutter, Ian began to turn purple in the face, his arm trembled and fell to his side, dropping the glass and spilling the contents squarely in his crotch.

The glass fell to the foul carpet and rolled to one side as Ian watched, bug-eyed.

"He's choking!" Someone at the table shouted and jumped up to punch him in the back.

The thumping sound brought Emily out of her trance and she looked Ian in the face. His colour was returning to normal; he looked down at the wet patch on his jeans. "Get off me!" he yelled to the first-aider and slapped her away. "And you..." He stabbed a chubby finger towards Emily, struggling for words, "...you can fuck off!" And with that bestowal of eloquence, he stormed back to the bar whereupon the others pointed at the stain and laughed.

Mads, lost for words just stared at Emily with her mouth half open. "What just happened?" she muttered.

Emily shrugged, genuinely none the wiser and stepped over to the table, picked up what she assumed was Mads' glass and downed the remainder. She wiped her mouth with the back of her hand and smiled across the table, "Thanks Mike."

Mike chortled and raised his glass as Emily led Mads towards the exit.

As she turned, her eye caught a group through the archway to the snug. The light was low, but she could make out a woman at a table flanked by a pair of gaunt-looking men. Both African, or maybe Jamaican but so sickly looking that their skin appeared a ghastly grey.

A third man seemed to be pleading to the woman, it was hard to make out her features in the shadows. Suddenly, one of her associates slammed the man's head against the table. He slumped to the ground whimpering. At that moment, and for a fraction of a second the woman's ancient eyes made contact with Emily's and she was sure there was a flash of light between them.

A sensation like icy water poured down her spine. She looked away and hurried outside into the cold.

"I thought we'd seen the last of those idiots," Emily said to Mads, her breath now forming ephemeral wisps of white.

"Nah, they're here every night it seems. Not one of them has done a day's work since school."

"I don't think we've done a lot better," Emily sighed.

"Hey, chicken, we're getting there." She stroked the back of Emily's head, "We've got our own place, we pay our way. Maybe that English A-Level might be worth something if I can ever get started on that novel."

Emily scoffed, and took her hand, "One day, Mads."

They started walking out of the car park, hand in hand carefully avoiding the worst of the broken glass which crunched underfoot like ice.

Without warning, the two gaunt gentlemen who were with the old woman inside stepped out from the alleyway next to the pub. They blocked the path in front of the girls, standing as solid as concrete posts.

They were as thin as sticks, the expensive looking suits they wore hung off them like rags. Emily shuddered, they looked for all the world like corpses dressed in their funeral clothes.

Mads had to look up a little to address the one in front of her such was his height. "Um, mate–" she managed before she was grabbed by the arm and pushed back a step. For such a frail guy, his grip was like steel. She yelped, he released her and glared down at her with dull, cloudy eyes.

The woman from the pub stepped from the alley and approached Emily through the blockade. She looked her up and down slowly with eyes sunken into her dark, shrivelled face. The enormous fur coat that engulfed her was festooned with strange trinkets and symbols.

She licked her lips and when she spoke, it was dry as dust, slow and heavily accented creole.

"You got a *smell* 'bout you, girl." She reached out with a bony hand and held Emily's chin, turning her head to examine her, like fruit in the marketplace.

Mads lunged to try to pull the woman's hand away

but was met with a backhand slap from the nearest bodyguard that felt like an iron bar. She staggered back, checking her face for blood. "You let her go!" she yelled.

"I see what you are, girl," the woman continued, ignoring what had just happened. Emily was too terrified to move; her breath came out in little puffs of white, her eyes wide with fear.

A car passed by. The woman's eyes swivelled to watch it turn a corner and disappear, then back to Emily.

"Come." She said simply, and turned and walked back into the alley. Emily could have made a break for it, but instead, she found herself following before she had even realised what was happening.

She was only vaguely aware of the commotion behind her as the two zombies pushed Mads along behind her. She knew now that was what they were, it was clear that they could only be the dead.

There was a little light in the alley from an emergency sign above the pub's fire exit, and in the green light she saw the woman's eyes boring into hers.

In the hard shadows of the little light, all Emily could see were the whites of the woman's eyes against the ebony blackness of her skin, like the fiery discs of distant suns, burning in the void of space. They seemed now to be producing a light of their own, the rest of the world had darkened and not so much vanished in her peripheral vision as become *irrelevant*.

Suddenly, she realised that she was being held in some kind of trance, she became aware of her own body again and could feel the life being slowly drawn from it as a spider might drain the vital fluids from its prey.

Her heart began to race, she still had little perception of the world outside her own body and those eyes into which her life was pouring. A rage began to build in her, like the distant sound of a great wave; the rushing sound drawing closer, until with a crash it enveloped her with a blinding white light.

The light rapidly expanded out from her in a bubble, fading as it rushed away, but behind it, the world flooded back in.

"...go of her, you're killing her you bitch!" came Mads' voice. She was somehow aware of her behind, being held by the two henchmen.

The woman had staggered back with the force of the expanding energy bubble, a look between incredulity and terror on her face.

"Ah, now don' you be tryin' 'dat girl." She snarled, raising both her hands palm-first towards Emily. A wave-front of blue erupted from those gnarled digits only to be met by another white-hot bubble of energy from somewhere within Emily. She had no comprehension of what it was, or how she was doing this; it felt like some kind of reflex, something almost primal.

Where the two forces met, the air tore into plasma with a slow, cracking, ripping sound. Then everything was the sound of screaming, the woman bellowing in pain, anger, humiliation. Mads caught in the blast, the two zombies wheezed and snarled, all to be joined by Emily's own cry of pain and surprise.

Then still, and darkness.

It was unusual for the doorbell to ring so early in the morning.

"You're not expecting a delivery are you, love?" Emily's mum dried her hands on a tea towel, folded it neatly and placed it on the kitchen worktop then hurried into the hallway.

Emily's dad grunted something into his coffee.

A few seconds later, her mum's head appeared around the kitchen door. She spoke slowly and carefully. "Emily, darling. A... *friend* is here to see you." She glared at her father with a significant look. He stopped chewing his toast, shrugged then carried on, disinterested.

"For me?" Emily stood, dragging her chair noisily across the tiled floor.

"I left her outside, she's... well, she's certainly an unusual sort," she laughed nervously.

There was no doubt that it was Mads, besides who else *could* it be, she didn't have any other friends.

Emily opened the door to the beaming face of Madeline. Straight away, she produced Emily's bag with a flourish.

"Oh my God, Mads, my bag!" she squealed with delight and took it.

"I hope I got everything,"

"Looks like it," Emily replied, rummaging about inside. Then she closed it and turned it about this way and that, her face fell. "Except–"

"Yeah, about that."

"Cat?"

"Um, Ian. He–"

"The shit-bag!" Emily spat, then glanced back into the house. Her parents didn't approve of bad language. Truth be told, they didn't approve of very much.

"I managed to get a lot of the pieces, but not all." She pulled her own bag off her shoulder and reached inside. "I made this from what was left. Look, I don't know if it's appropriate, maybe I'm being a bit forward or creepy or–"

"What! You made this?" Emily grabbed the little cloth doll and held it to her chest. "You made this for *me*?" Her dark eyes were gleaming.

"That's the best one, made another but it wasn't very good." She smiled, a little bashful. Big, stocky, tough Mads – bashful. She'd gotten it *bad*, that was sure.

"Thanks, Mads. It's just perfect." She held it up to study it properly. The stitching was neatly done. It wasn't much bigger than her outstretched hand, but the little arms and legs, plump tummy were cute. It was the face that had taken Emily's breath away, because what had once been a two-tone calico cat was now a clearly recognisable caricature of the wonderful young woman on her doorstep. The two colours of cloth sewn exactly to match her own portwine birthmark, little twists of wool for her short cropped white hair. Only the eyes were different. Shiny black beads where Mads' green eyes would have been.

A cheeky thought crept into Emily's mind and she leaned forwards to whisper, "I can finally take you to bed with me tonight."

Mads burst out in a massive belly-laugh.

"Is everything okay?" Emily's mum called from the kitchen.

"Oh. Yeah, all fine Mum. Um, Madeline here found my bag for me. I lost it yesterday."

"You lost it?" Her mum appeared suddenly from behind the door, making Mads jump back slightly. Emily hid the doll behind the bag. Her parents both had some very old-fashioned views; Mads certainly fell into several categories they would struggle with. The revelation that they were now very likely 'a thing' would quite possibly have sent them to their graves.

Emily's mum eyed Mads suspiciously, "Well, that's very kind of you Madeline." she enunciated a little in deference to her... she forced a smile while she tried to work out exactly what to make of her. *She had a bit of an accent, so she must be foreign or some such thing. And oh, the poor girl, how did she come by such a terrible scar? Was it a burn, an accident? It looked painful.*

An awkward moment passed, then Emily piped up, "Mads, just wait a moment will you?" She darted inside, leaving her mum with her increasingly strained smile.

Mads smiled sweetly back, pretended to take an interest in the wisteria growing around the door.

Emily appeared suddenly from the door, toast hanging from her mouth and a hairbrush in her hand.

"Bye Mum, see you tonight." Then, tapping Mads' shoulder, "Come on then, let's go," She powered off up the street. Mads turned and waved back at Emily's mum who weakly reciprocated before peering left and right out of the door and disappearing back inside.

"Well, that was awkward." Mads said, trotting up from behind.

"Yeah, sorry, my parents are a bit weird."

They walked in silence for a few moments, while Emily digested the minutes that had just passed.

"I really appreciate what you've done. I mean, with those boys yesterday, chasing them off, getting all my stuff." She stopped and turned to Mads, "I didn't even know you could sew!"

"Yeah, my mum taught me years ago, you know, when she was alive." She turned and they carried on walking into the park.

"Look, I know we've been really into each other this last week, and I – well, I don't know where things might have gone yesterday but..." she paused, hardly daring to ask in case she was wrong. "Well, I kind of think this all changes things a little. Is this really *it*? Are we really a *thing*?"

"Damn, girl!" Mads cried in a put-on creole accent, "I should hope so, I was up 'till dawn working on that doll!" They laughed and Mads bumped shoulders with Emily nearly knocking her over.

As they approached the shabby-looking band-stand, Emily hopped up onto one of the steps and stopped Mads. She was a good head taller than Emily, she stared intently into her lush green eyes. Mads tilted her head slightly.

"You know, until I saw you I really didn't know who I was." Emily spoke softly, her long hair moving slightly in the warm breeze. "I hadn't even thought about whether I wanted a boyfriend, or even a girlfriend. I never even thought about boys at all..." she paused, a slight flush bloomed under her eyes, "Even when I... you know."

Mads laughed, "You gotta think about *something* to get you going."

"I do now," she admitted, "I just wish we'd have had the time together yesterday, I didn't even get to ki–"

Silently, Mads had moved closer, and in that moment, her lips brushed against Emily's, making the very word she was set to utter, flesh. Softly, she kissed her; so very gently. For someone built so powerfully, Madeline had the softest touch, and it thrilled Emily to the marrow.

With every ounce of resolve, she resisted dragging this big, beautiful girl behind the rusting bandstand and letting everything go. She closed her eyes and let Madeline kiss her with a tenderness that she had hardly believed possible.

A faint croaking sound was coming from the old woman. She was laying on her side about twenty paces from where Emily lay on her back. Her vision swam and flickered with blobs of coloured light. Try as she might, she was unable to move; every part of her body was numb.

"Angelo, Lucius!" came the croaking again, muffled in Emily's hearing, "Get to me now, you damn fools."

But her calls went unheeded. The two undead were for the most part unharmed by the psychic blasts that ripped through the narrow alleyway. The girls and the old woman were knocked out, but possessing no real, natural consciousness and certainly no intelligence to speak of, the two idiot corpses continued to shuffle aimlessly about – but now, injured and weak, the old woman had no control over them. Like a pair of clockwork toys, they bumped randomly around, until by chance they found their way out onto the road and were gone into the freezing night.

Emily tried to call out to Madeline to see if she was okay, but the effort to speak caused her vision to dim further and a feeling like she might vomit.

In the moments before she blacked out again, she sensed a presence by her side, moving, a hand touched her side – was it Mads? She tried to turn her head but her eyes burst with orange blobs of colour. There was a tugging sensation at her side. What did it mean? Again, one large tug and she realised that someone had snatched *Little Mads* from her belt.

The last she knew, was the sound of an approaching police car and a return to blackness.

CHAPTER 4

A SMALL CROWD had gathered to gawk at the sideshow put on by the ambulances. Now they had driven away, the onlookers had put away their phones and evaporated into the night.

Earlier, when the detonation in the alleyway had shaken the pub windows, the occupants tumbled out to imvestigate..

Ryan lit up a cigarette and took a deep draw, snorting twin gouts of smoke from his nose.

"Give." The girl at his side whined, "C'mon, giz a drag."

He took another long draw and passed the cigarette over. "Got to be lightning," he muttered, downing the last of the beer he'd taken out with him.

"Can't be," the girl sighed. "Told ya – no rain." She gestured upwards with the glowing fag-tip, "No clouds."

"Fucked if I know then," he grumbled.

The pub door swung open and a figure in a shabby hoodie wandered out, looked about furtively then made his way over to Ryan.

"Mate," he slurred. Ryan took a small step back; the guy reeked, "You seen Juliana? She ain't in her spot." He scratched absently at his hip, looking about. "Barman said something about a shooting... wasn't her was it? 'Cos, like I need to *see* her."

Ryan waved the junkie on, "No, bruh, no idea where she is. Just two bloody dykes got taken out."

The junkie groaned and ambled away muttering to himself.

Ryan shook his head, then seemed to remember his glass, empty but for a gob of foam. "Let's get back in. Freezing my nuts off now. Time for another, I reckon."

The girl flicked the cigarette butt away to join the foul heap of others in the concrete ring and followed enthusiastically behind.

"Funny little thing," the nurse remarked placing the doll on the table beside Emily's bed. "Is it a character from a video game or something? Pavel, you know about these kind of things."

The young porter picked it up and turned it about, "Nothing I've ever seen. Manga perhaps?"

"Oh, now you've lost me," the nurse clucked, taking the figure from the lad and placing it carefully back.

"But It's special to her, that's for sure." She stopped to look back at the comatose girl in the darkened room, before turning to leave. "They had to prise it from her hand when they brought her in."

The door to the ICU room closed softly behind them. In the warm darkness, the lights and traces of the monitoring machines quietly and dutifully kept watch.

At the nurses' station, the lights were low and darkness filled the wards to either side. Patients mostly slept; one groaned gently despite the fervent embrace of morphia.

"Strange case in ITU three." The doctor spoke in hushed tones which only served to accentuate his rich baritone voice. "Came in not two hours ago covered in burns, but now..." He placed a pair of mugs onto the desk. The nurse smiled and accepted one. "Now, just a little redness, a few minor abrasions."

"Did the ambulance crew make a mistake booking her in?" The nurse sipped at the warming brew.

"No, I was still on shift when they were brought in. I saw the damage." He scratched at the beginnings of a beard and looked over the notes again.

"What about the other girl?" she asked, "They've not brought her down yet."

The doctor looked up from the papers and shook his head slowly. The nurse's shoulders fell, "Oh. Oh, that's very sad."

"Burns," he said simply, "Pretty bad, but I think it was electrical shock that did the real damage. Never really came out of VF for more than a minute or two. Heart just gave up on her in the end."

There was an uncomfortable silence for a couple of seconds. The doctor broke it first. "Righto then. Paperwork, then that's me done." He smiled weakly and raised his mug as he turned to leave.

"You in tomorrow?" the nurse called after him.

He smiled to himself and called back over his shoulder, "For my sins, yes. Noon." Then he was gone through the heavy, swinging door.

A trained eye would have noticed the subtle change in the *beep-beep* of Emily's monitors, a quickening of the pulse-rate, a change in her breathing, her body temperature. But most would recognise the darting of her eyes beneath their lids as signs that she was dreaming. Apart from that, the room was still, no sounds except the monitor and a tiny hiss of oxygen from the breathing tube snaking from her mouth.

If there were an observer in the room, a loved one keeping vigil over the stricken girl, they would have jumped when the little doll on the table slumped and fell to one side with a gentle thump.

But they would have laughed it off. A breeze? Had they kicked the table earlier? They might have picked it up and sat it up neatly and thought no more of it.

What they would have done when the leg of the little figure twitched once, and again... well that's anyone's guess.

The little calico doll swung merrily from Emily's rucksack as she strode through the school gates, Mads at her side. She dared to touch her hand briefly, and Mads stroked her index finger with her thumb and turned to smile.

Emily's little heart was beating fast and strong in her chest. This feeling was like nothing she had ever experienced in her life, it felt like fear, but sweet as cotton candy, like an unexplored land that she knew she had lived a lifetime in in her dreams.

A boy pushed rudely past, bumping her shoulder. It was Ryan.

"F'kin lezzers!" He scowled over his shoulder, then directly to Emily, his face contorted with disgust, "Freak!"

Ian dashed to catch up with him and they exchanged a few secret words as they powered away.

He stopped and turned several paces in front, forcing the girls to halt in the busy flow of students pouring past. He seemed to be trying to think of something to say, but the words eluded him. Finally in frustration he spat "Witch!"

Mads shouted and feigned a punch at the boy. He flipped them a middle finger and turned to catch up with Ryan.

"Just ignore them," Emily said, "they're just little boys."

Ahead of them, Ian howled with laughter at something Ryan was showing him on his phone.

Mads scoffed, "It's no wonder I don't like boys." She started off again, "That little doll's got more between its ears than the lot of them." She flicked it and it bounced about again, looking like it didn't have a care in the world. "You gonna give it a name? I mean you can't call it Cat anymore."

Emily thought for a moment as they reached the pair of large glass doors to the main building. A smile spread over her face and she held the heavy door open to let *her girlfriend* enter – the phrase sent a tingle down her spine.

"*Little Mads,*" she announced grandly, doffing her head like a doorman as Mads passed by, "I'll call her *Little Mads.*"

The pair separated to go to their respective tutor groups, then either last-ditch lessons or study periods to prepare for their exams. Mads had her A-levels next week, so was working every hour she could. Emily thought about the precious revision time that she must have sacrificed for her last night and felt a tug in her heart while she stared hopelessly at a past maths paper she was practicing on. Little Mads sat on the desk, her shiny eyes seemingly looking up at her in encouragement.

She only had a couple of weeks until her own GCSE exams began, and she *knew* that she wasn't ready. Her recent PPE or *mock* exam results were dismal, projected grades nowhere near enough to consider taking A-levels in September. She was on a damage-limitation plan now. Perhaps, with some hard work over the summer, and some tutoring she might be able to re-sit?

The maths question with its attendant graph continued to taunt her until the signal sounded for lunch. She shoved the contents of the desk wearily into her bag and clipped Little Mads back onto her cute little carabiner.

The school canteen had prepared a fairly reasonable

attempt at a curry, though the rice was watery and sat on the plate with a small puddle of milky seepage around it.

She was hoping that Mads would be there; she really needed to just be with her after the fruitless morning she had endured.

"Hey, little Chicken!" A soft voice in her ear from behind. Mads! Oh, thank God. She stifled a squeal and turned to see, almost knocking the older girl's tray from her hands.

She beamed. Then a quizzical face, "Chicken? Huh?"

Mads sat down at the little table with her tray and began unloading the plate, cutlery, drink from it. "Yeah. While we're making up little nicknames..." She reached and placed the tray against the leg of the table.

"I don't get it." Still beaming, drinking in the features of Mads' face.

"Um. I'll tell you later, it's *filthy!*" She smirked and looked at her own curry as if she'd made a terrible error of judgement.

Emily saw Mads' eyes flick to the graphic novel laying open on the table beside her.

"Have you read *Rising Flesh?*" Emily asked.

"Shit Girl, every damn one!" Mads face lit up and she leaned in. "You read the *last* one?"

"About a thousand times. It's genius."

"You know he died recently, the artist, Jake Mayer, just before the ep. was released?" Mads asked conspiratorially.

"I do. And I don't believe a word of what they said

about it. I think he was on to something and they bumped him off."

Mads took a gulp of lukewarm Vimto and grimaced "What makes you think that?"

"He left signs," Emily said, eyes fixed on Mads' "They're all through the book."

"Signs?"

Across the canteen a group of students burst out laughing, one of the girls shrieked.

"Take a look. Every spread, there's a paw-print hidden somewhere. Sometimes they're really hard to find but they're there!"

Mads shrugged, "Maybe he just likes dogs?"

Whatever the joke was, it was starting to spread. Here and there the chime of social media apps rang out to be followed by gasps or stifled laughter. Mads looked up to see what the commotion was then shook her head dismissively.

"Maybe," Emily sighed, "I guess we'll never know now."

Without warning, and from out of nowhere a cocktail sausage, impaled on a little wooden chip fork bounced off the middle of the table and landed on Emily's plate spattering her with the remains of her lunch. From across the canteen some smart-alec struck up a short air-guitar riff.

At that, the entire canteen erupted into a chaos of derisive laughter. A group of boys had got up on their chairs and were waving their pinkie fingers, chanting something that neither girl could make out over the din.

Emily realised with a horror that threatened to

swallow her up in icy blackness what had just happened.

Mads jumped to her feet and began raging, shouting incandescent obscenities at the one table of boys who had remained sitting.

A hot rage swept through Emily, though she struggled to move such was the utter depth of her humiliation. The video taken at the sanctuary was now broadcast for the world to see – yesterday's humiliation was *not* complete, it was only the start.

The sounds of the uproar and Mads' yells began to distort and muffle like she was close to passing out. Just before the inferno in her head consumed her, ICE.

Water suddenly drenched her, cold and furious. Her eyes snapped open and the world flooded back in. The laughter and taunts had turned to screams, sounds of chairs being knocked over as the students crushed and clamoured to escape the downpour of the sprinklers.

Still dazed, she was vaguely aware of Mads taking her by the arm and leading her outside to safety.

Nurse Parker eyed the monitor at her desk as the rhythms returned back to normal. She had almost elected to leave the comfort of her desk to investigate when the storm began to subside.

The last of her hot chocolate was cold now and contained nasty gritty bits, but she drained the mug and returned to her paperwork.

"Something's scared you my lovely," she whispered, "something frightful."

She hadn't noticed on the CCTV that the little fabric doll that had been lying on the table earlier had gone.

CHAPTER 5

A WEAK AFTERNOON sun seeped through the blinds in
Emily's room, the ancient, gurgling radiator by the
window fending off the chill outside.

Her hair had been arranged neatly by the morning
staff who had cleaned her, checked the drips and
monitors, noted her condition. She might have been
in peaceful slumber were it not for the ribbed plastic
tube protruding from her mouth, hissing rhythmically
accompanied by the soft, steady beat of the monitor
to her side.

Her eyes, restless from earlier nightmares were still
again; long black lashes bowed in sleep.

Without warning, her eyes snapped open, darting
wildly about in panic.

The monitor screamed in alarm giving shrill voice to Emily's muted choking. She gagged and her hands flew to the pipe snaking out from her mouth but found it firmly taped in place.

Choking, her forced breaths whistling through the pipes and machinery she scrabbled and clawed at the tape.

At that instant, the doors burst open and two hospital staff crashed though and fell upon the frantic patient.

One held her hands away while the other carefully withdrew the tube from her throat. It seemed to go on forever, finally it was out with a rasping cough.

Tears of shock and pain streamed from Emily's eyes which had rolled back to reveal the whites as she drew a long and painful breath then coughed long and hard.

The first attendant – a plump woman – working with quick, efficient movements pushed a syringe of clear liquid into one of the lines attached to Emily's arm. Slowly she began to relax, her breathing slowed and her lids drooped a little over her dark eyes.

"There we go, my lovely," It was nurse Parker, still on duty from a shift that had begun... she wasn't even sure when now. "That's right, just breathe normally."

Emily tried to speak but the pain in her throat stopped her.

"No, don't try to speak for a bit. It's going to be sore for a while. We had to put a tube in you to help you breathe."

Emily's eyes turned to nurse Parker, questioningly.

"You're going to be okay my lovely," she soothed. "Good. You're doing just fine." Then, to the junior nurse, "Lorna, would you page Dr Franklin. He'll want to come see Miss Moon.

Despite the sedative, Emily's lips were still moving, mouthing a word over and over. She coughed again and finally managed to rasp, "Mads. Were... where's Mads?"

Nurse Parker held Emily's hand gently, "Just rest for now. The doctor will be here soon."

"I– what happened to Mads?" Emily struggled; her throat was raw. "She was hurt... a flash." The effort to speak was exhausting; her head slumped back into the pillow.

In all her years dealing with patients and their families, the job of breaking awful news never got any easier. Prolonging the moment for as long as possible, she looked about the room and noticed the little cloth doll.

"Oh, how did you get down there? Sorry, my love we must have knocked it off the table when we were sorting your tubes out." She let go of Emily's hand which flopped to the mattress and retrieved the doll from where it lay under the bulky hospital bed. "I'll just pop it back up here for you." She propped it up back on the table, squeezing it gently so that the beans in the body flowed and allowed it to sit neatly.

To her relief, Dr Franklin stepped into the room; he smelled freshly showered despite being many hours into his long shift.

He saw that Nurse Parker had noticed, and was beaming at him.

"Just come out of theatre," he offered to the unasked question. "Lad from early this morning." He sighed;

he'd hardly had a break since he started again this morning. The lad needed more surgery after the emergency team had patched him up and it had been touch and go for a while – he still wasn't out of the woods yet. But he couldn't discuss a patient in front of another. He'd make some excuse to visit the nurses' station afterwards.

Nurse Parker handed him the clipboard which had been hanging from the foot of the bed. He scanned it silently while Emily eyed him nervously, looking for any signal on his face that might indicate his prognosis.

He made to hand it back, glanced one more time at it and sucked his teeth.

"Miss Moon–" he began, stepping to the head of the bed and smiling down at the stricken form.

"Emily." She inserted weakly.

The doctor smiled warmly, "Of course. Emily. How are you feeling?"

Slightly thrown by being asked questions when what she really wanted was answers, she stumbled for a moment to take stock. "Um. Okay, I guess." Was the honest answer, "A bit of a headache, feel like I've run a marathon." She paused to rub her throat, "Throat's sore," she finished.

"Yes, sorry about that. That one's on us I'm afraid, but perfectly normal. You'll be fine in a couple of days." He stopped, looked her in the eyes. "Other than that?"

"No. Nothing really."

The doctor seemed to be at odds with something, and that began to frighten Emily.

"Is it okay if I examine you, just your neck and arms? Your back if you're able to sit up for me?"

Emily nodded quietly, and with a little effort sat up in bed.

Quietly, the doctor lifted the hair from her neck. Gently squeezed, then lifted her arms one at a time and looked along her pale skin.

"Just going to undo the back of your gown," he advised. The only sound he made was a simple "Mm-hm," before stepping back to allow Nurse parker to re-tie her. She raised the bed up to a more comfortable sitting position and guided her back.

"Well," he began, "The good news is that you do indeed seem to be perfectly well."

"I'm sensing a 'but'?"

"No. Not really. Except..." He paused, unsure, "When you were brought in last night, you presented with what looked like some very nasty burns. Electrical?" He parted his hands, "But now, there don't seem to be any signs of that at all."

Emily looked at her arms; definitely no burns there.

"Your face too."

Emily put her hand to her cheek.

"No, that's gone. But there was a distinct reddening down one side... you ever seen the movie *Close Encounters of the Third Kind*?"

Emily nodded again and sniffed.

"I can't really explain how even mild burns would have healed up completely overnight."

Emily looked back at him, blinking.

"Do you remember what happened at all?"

The events of the evening came rushing back like a

tsunami of images and feelings – the alleyway, the old lady, blinding light, darkness, some kind of struggle, flashes from her nightmare, feelings of anger, then something that she couldn't comprehend, searching for something or someone, anger again, triumph, then ending with one last picture of Mads lying on her side, back to her. Motionless.

"MADS!" she shouted snapping to, "Where is she? I need to see her!" Her eyes were streaming with tears and she trembled feebly.

Doctor Franklin pursed his lips and drew a long breath through his nose.

The screaming could be clearly heard through the thin wall that separated the two intensive treatment rooms. The patient next door wasn't troubled by the sounds though. In his inert state, the anguished cries were of no consequence.

Ryan lay motionless, connected to his own monitors, the large dressing on his neck slightly stained from a stubborn seepage of blood and fluids from the catastrophic wounds inflicted on him the night before.

Franklin's work seemed to be holding though.

"She can't be!" Emily was yelling and thrashing about on the bed, while Nurse Parker tried her best to soothe and restrain her, stop her hurting herself and those around her.

"She was just next to me, look!" She held out her forearm to Dr Franklin, then to Nurse Parker, who nodded and smiled weakly. "I'm fine, how can she be... how can she be dead? Not Mads, please no." She slumped forwards heaving deeply, sobbing.

Nurse Parker loosened her hold and gently stroked her arm as the convulsions slowly subsided.

Eventually, Emily pulled the hair from her face; strands remained stuck to her cheek. She accepted a tissue from the nurse and cleared her nose.

"How?" she repeated, hoarsely to Dr Franklin.

"We're pretty sure it was her heart. An underlying condition. We were able to detect it by ultrasound while we were treating her – just a preliminary diagnosis of course, we... we can check to be sure."

"She never said she was sick. Her *heart*? But she was always so fit, she ran almost every day."

Franklin nodded sombrely, "Yes. I don't think she would have known. What she had, *Hypertrophic cardiomyopathy* – sometimes called 'athlete's heart' – is not uncommon in athletes as the name suggests. It can go undetected for years, no symptoms, then..."

"Like that footballer?" Emily asked, taking another tissue from a box that Nurse Parker had placed in her lap.

"The same. It's a genetic condition." He sighed, genuinely sad for Emily's loss, "Just strikes out of the blue."

A few moments passed, while Emily sniffed miserably.

"Look," Dr Franklin resumed, "You seem like you're on the mend, so I'd like to move you to one of the quiet, general wards. We'll keep you in overnight for observations to make sure and then you can go home in the morning. How does that sound?"

Emily reached out to the table, "I want Little Mads.

Don't leave her behind when they move me."

The doctor smiled and picked up the little figure from the table. As he did, a brief flicker of shock registered as he connected the resemblance in the little face to the girl he'd fought so hard to save earlier.

"You were close, weren't you? She had you listed as her next of kin." He passed the doll to Emily who clutched it to her face and sniffed deeply.

Amongst the sago beans were a few coffee beans, the smell reminded her of Mads' penchant for expensive coffees whenever they had a few pounds to spare. That was her biggest vice.

"All we had in this world were each other," she said in a faraway voice.

"If you like, you can see her, say goodbye."

The beans inside little Mads rustled as Emily stiffened and looked up to the doctor, eyes brimming with tears. She tried to speak, but only a whimper came. "I don't know," she managed at last, "I just don't know what to do next."

A few moments passed while Franklin seemed to be wrestling with a decision.

"Nurse Parker, would you let us have the room for a moment?"

The nurse nodded quietly, smiled sweetly at Emily and swept quietly out of the room. A few more seconds passed before Franklin spoke.

"Emily. Please forgive me if this is inappropriate, or too soon but there's a wonderful opportunity for you to help us."

Emily looked up from Little Mads, who now sat in her lap seemingly looking up. "Of course." Her voice was tiny and fragile now, and the thought that she might be willing to help someone else even at this time brought a lump to Franklin's throat.

"Let me explain." He dragged a plastic chair to the side of the bed and sat. "We're a teaching hospital. We work with the local university to develop new techniques, medicines, understanding."

Emily nodded; it all sounded very noble.

"There's one particular young lady who is working on her doctorate who might be very interested in talking with you."

"About my skin healing so quickly?" Emily guessed, turning her arm about to look for any remaining signs of burns – there were of course none.

Franklin chuckled briefly, "No, though I think there's a doctorate's thesis in that alone if the truth be told. No," he shuffled slightly in his seat, a little uneasy. "While we were treating you... we put in all the tubes and things, we needed to catheterise you."

Of course, Emily was no medical expert, but she was a big fan of *Casualty* on BBC TV and recognised the term. She realised why Dr Franklin seemed a little embarrassed, even for a doctor.

"Ah yes, I know what you're getting at," she said, brightening a little, "It's okay, there's nothing to be embarrassed about." It was *her* time now to reassure him, "I don't mind talking about it."

Franklin seemed to relax a little, "Thank you. I'm sorry if this is a little personal. So, we have a student working on her doctorate and she's writing a thesis on urology and reproductive conditions. Your particular condition is exactly what she has asked me to look out for."

Emily's dark eyes were fixed on Franklin's now, fascinated. Franklin pushed on, encouraged by her apparent interest.

"Would it be okay if I allowed the student, her name's Kelley by the way, to speak with you, with your permission examine you? There's absolutely no obligation." But before he had finished speaking, Emily was nodding.

"Yes. I'd be fine with that," she said simply, "I've never spoken to a doctor or anything about this, even when I was little. My parents just wanted to ignore it, pretend that I was normal. I'd like to learn about myself too."

Again, the lump in Franklin's throat rose and he pretended to be checking some notes for a second or two. "That's. That's very kind of you Emily," he said eventually. "What's more, I understand that the university has a heathy budget for volunteers, so I expect that you would be paid for your time."

He rose; the plastic chair scraping noisily as he did so, "Thank you again. I'll go let our student know and then she can get in touch with you at some time to make arrangements."

The door bumped closed behind him and Emily was alone again in the room. The light through the window was taking on beautiful orange and peach hues as the sun began to take its leave of the day in the late winter afternoon.

"Well, Little Mads," she said with a little cheer in her tiny voice, "That's a bonus at least." She lay back on the propped-up bed and engulfed herself in the huge array of pillows. It had been the worst of all days, now she needed a little time to begin to process how the rest of her life was going to pan out without her precious Mads.

Emily must have dozed off, but not for long as a ruddy light still flowed into the room as the door opened and Dr Franklin peered around.

"Emily. Hello again. Well, it seems that you're certainly of interest in the study." He opened the door and stepped inside, followed by a young lady carrying a laptop case. "Allow me to introduce you to Kelley Stranack."

CHAPTER 6

KELLEY STRODE INTO the room, hand outstretched for a handshake that Emily found herself powerless to refuse. Her hand was soft and warm, and despite the aura of powerful confidence she exuded as she approached, her grip was gentle, almost comforting.

Immediately, Emily felt that this was somebody that she could trust, even with the things which she had kept hidden for most of her life.

Dr Franklin silently flashed an 'ok' gesture to Kelley and backed out of the door to attend to his other patients.

Kelley sat and put her tablet onto the bedside table, pausing for a fraction of a second to eye Little Mads who was propped up against a plastic jug of water.

She appeared to nod, perhaps to herself for some reason and then turned her attention to Emily.

"Emily. Thank you *so* much for offering to volunteer to help my study. It's not often that we find cases such as yours, and even then those subjects are, quite understandably not so keen to talk about it."

Emily's eyes were transfixed on Kelley as she spoke. But as she broke for breath, her eyes darted to the little doll on the table. She reached out for it and held it tightly, she wanted to know more but the prospect of baring all was a gigantic leap to make.

Kelley seemed to sense this and leaned a little closer to speak with a lower tone, "But if at any time you don't feel comfortable," she spread he hands, "just let me know and we can slow down or even stop completely. Is that okay?"

Emily nodded, her butterflies seemed to have simply evaporated leaving her feeling calm and in control.

"Great. So you'll be pleased to know that there won't be any need for an actual *physical* examination – no need to undress or anything. What I'd like to do is to is run an MRI scan on the lower part of your body so that I can take a good look inside and out without needing to trouble or embarrass you at all."

There was a definite sense of relief on her face when she heard that.

"Have you ever had an MRI?"

Emily shook her head.

"That's fine. There's really nothing to it at all. We'll just slide you into a big white doughnut, there will be all kind of funny noises and thumping sounds and it'll all be done."

"Sounds okay, I guess." Emily said, "When do we start?"

"Now, if you like," Kelley smiled warmly across the bed. She picked up her tablet and tapped a few times. "Here, if you can just read through these terms and scribble a signature at the bottom then we're good to go."

She handed the tablet over, and Emily started reading. There didn't seem to be too much there and the language wasn't hard to understand. "Looks like it's just privacy stuff..." she muttered as she slowly scrolled.

"Yeah." Kelley scoffed, "Data protection, disclaimers for stupid stuff; the usual." She got up and headed for the door, "I'll leave you with that for a couple of minutes while I fetch a porter."

"Por—?" Emily began, but when she looked up, she was alone.

It hadn't really occurred to her to wonder where all her stuff was from the other night until a little vibration hummed through the cabinet to her side. Her phone signalled the arrival of an email with her copy of the signed disclaimer just as the door bumped open a little clumsily.

A rather shabby-looking wheelchair pushed its way through, followed by a lanky young man at the handles. Kelley quietly swept into the room, around the porter and examined the tablet laying on the bed.

"Good. Any questions or concerns?"

"Um, do I really *need* a wheelchair? I think I feel okay enough to walk."

Kelley closed her eyes for a moment, "I'm afraid

so; the pen-pushers insist that all patients need to be in a chair or a bed when being moved around the hospital. Insurance reasons."

Emily shook her head and swung her legs out of the bed. Kelley offered her hand to help her down; it was quite high for the delicate girl.

Carefully adjusting her gown – the seat was cold – she made herself comfortable, with Little Mads in her lap. She looked up and grinned at Kelley, "Onwards."

There were two more rooms like Emily's before the big double doors that lead out into the lift lobby. As they passed the one next to hers, Emily felt strangely, uneasy. Gripping Little Mads, it felt like the beans under her cloth skin were squirming like insects.

The feeling passed as Kelley stopped suddenly in front of them and turned, her head cocked to one side.

"You okay?" she said with a serious voice.

"Just a little dizzy, I think." she looked over to the glass windows of the ITU, the blinds were shut tightly.

Kelley put a hand on Emily's knee and leaned in, "Don't worry about him. He's not going to be troubling anyone for quite some time."

Without warning, Emily's vision swam, and it felt to her like Little Mads was wriggling and struggling to climb out of her lap.

The next moment, the sensation was gone, and the little cloth doll was laying inert in her hands.

"See," Kelley glanced up at the young porter, then back again, "that's why you need a wheelchair."

It was quite a journey to the MRI unit. Two lift rides,

down a seemingly endless corridor and through a maze of shorter ones to the shiny new building.

The waiting room was clean; a water cooler and coffee vending machine stood against one wall.

There were two couples waiting there as well as a single patient with her mobile drip-stand.

A bored-looking porter glanced up from his phone for long enough to nod to Emily's steed, then leaned against the bed with his patient. The elderly woman coughed once through her plastic oxygen mask and raised her head feebly to see the new arrival.

"We can go right through for this abdo scan." Kelley said, briskly to the receptionist.

"Right through. Yes," came the reply.

Odd. Emily thought, the other patients looked like they needed their scans much more urgently than her. She wasn't even sick – at least not anymore.

"We can go now." Kelley turned to look at Emily. Yes, now Emily thought to herself. No reason not to. They wouldn't be long, what would another half an hour matter to the others in the waiting room.

"It's just the gown you have on, yes?" Kelley asked, once they were in the MRI machine room. Emily nodded. "And no jewellery, piercings... metal implants that we don't know about?" A vigorous shake of the head as Emily eyed the huge machine warily.

"Honestly, it doesn't hurt. It's just a little loud. I can give you some ear plugs if loud noises worry you."

"No, I'll be fine. I think I'm just a bit freaked out about finding out what's inside me."

Kelley, held out her hand and helped Emily up onto

the white patient table.

"You don't *have* to know if you don't want to."

A shrill beeping sound accompanied by hurried footsteps woke Emily from a deep and dreamless sleep. It took her a moment to remember where she was.

Someone rushed past in the corridor outside with a trolley, clattering and laden with medical equipment.

Something was happening in the room next to her, the one that had given her such a sense of unease.

A nurse was barking orders in hushed tones, then more hurried footsteps.

Terrified, Emily lay in her bed listening to the drama unfold, until one by one the voices became quiet. For a minute or two there was no sound, then a muttered exchange before the sounds of the staff next door dispersing, this time without the urgency from earlier.

It was clear to her what had happened next door. The patient had died. Had it been the same when they were fighting to save Mads? She felt about the bed for Little Mads, pulling the scratchy blanket about to see if she had become folded into it. Leaning over the side of he bed Emily spotted her precious keepsake on the floor again.

Somehow, she snagged one of the monitoring leads that snaked out of her gown, pulling it free from the monitor standing quiet vigil by her bed. Sensing the loss of some vital measurement, the screen lit calling its own distress as it's brother had done just a few minutes earlier.

In only seconds, the night nurse swept into the

room, quickly and silently as an owl might drop from the sky onto its prey.

Without a word, she silenced the machine and calmly reattached the lead to the sticky pad on Emily's chest.

"Thanks," Emily smiled up to the Nurse. "I was just trying to get my—"

"That's okay, precious. Just a wire came loose. You settle down and sleep now."

"What..." she knew the answer though, "What happened next door?"

The Nurse fussed over Emily's pillows for a moment, before walking around the bed to collect Little Mads from the floor, "Nothing for you to worry about now. Best get some sleep." She smiled and left.

The clattering sound of a cart woke Emily with a start – images from the night flashed before her eyes. She hadn't realised that she had slept, now the morning light was pouring into the room. Before she had the chance to wonder who was now being tended to by the emergency crash cart (she recalled the phrase from TV), the door burst open and a cheery faced woman shoved a trolley laden with trays, assorted breakfast foods and a gigantic urn.

"Tea, pet? Or would you prefer coffee?"

Emily realised that she was drawn up to the head of the bed with her knees pulled up to her chest. She looked up to the gigantic woman with her pale face and round black eyes.

"I've got a cooked breakfast here if you'd like one too?" She said, a little quieter.

Emily nodded, silently and slid her legs back down

while the woman pushed the table over the bed and busied herself pouring a mug of something hot.

A covered plastic tray joined the mug of tea and when the lid was pulled away, the scent of cooked breakfast almost made Emily reel. She hadn't for a moment considered that she might be hungry – when was the last time she ate? Was it Boxing Day now? It must be.

"Turkey sausages, pet," the woman... Margaret, she read on her badge, said noticing Emily regarding the plate thoughtfully.

"Healthier – so I'm told." She had the air of someone who was impossibly busy, and yet she had the time for a kindly smile. "Is that all okay for you?"

Emily nodded again, still a little overwhelmed.

"What day is it?" Emily managed, shifting into a more comfortable position and pulling the table a little closer.

"It's Tuesday, my love," beamed the catering lady. Emily wished the dinner ladies at her school had been so cheerful. "Funny to have another bank holiday on a Tuesday, but with Christmas on the Sunday its a bit of a win... for most, that don't have to work."

"Oh," Emily realised that she'd missed a day, "I thought it was Boxing Day today."

The woman, chuckled. "Oh bless your heart. I always count Christmas a success if I can forget what day it is."

The door creaked open and a head poked through.

"Look, you've got a visitor. I'll be back later for your plate."

Kelley slid through the door and held it wide open

for the woman to negotiate her cart back outside. She left with a "cheerio" and disappeared, with a hum and a clank down the corridor.

"Hey." Kelley's soft voice seemed to lessen Emily's anxiety. She pulled up a chair and watched as Emily devoured one of the sausages that she'd impaled on a fork.

"Sorry," Emily managed through a mouthful of sausage, "Just *so* hungry."

"That's okay. You carry on, I can talk while you eat if that's okay?

"Mm-hmm."

Kelley chuckled, "Okay, that's fine." She pulled her tablet out from her shoulder bag and tapped on it a couple of times. "Dr Franklin has kindly let me stand in for him this morning and give you all the good news."

Emily paused, a forkful of scrambled egg hovering half way to her ravenous mouth.

"I need some good news," she said weakly, and engulfed the egg.

Kelley nodded, "Yes, I know. Well the good news is that you're completely fine. Dr Franklin is happy for you to go home today as soon as you feel you're able."

"Really?" A smile, for the first time, "Oh, that's brilliant." Her face fell.

Kelley caught the situation before it turned bad. "Yes. Madeline. I'm so sorry about that. The hospital can arrange for you to see a councillor to help you through the times ahead if you need."

Emily prodded a half a grilled tomato with her fork

but decided that the slightly flaccid bacon slice was more to her appetite.

"Or we can just talk if you like," Kelley offered warmly, "I'm not actually trained, but I'm a good listener."

Emily turned her head, eyes overflowing with tears.

In the moment it took Kelley to jump from the plastic chair and throw her arms around her, Emily had broken down into deep shuddering sobs. He had witnessed death twice in as many days, and now she was alone.

She wept into Kelley's long, red hair. The few breaths she took were ragged and she smelled her coconut shampoo. It was somehow comforting, she could feel the pitiful pain and loss slowly ebb from her body, as if she were just letting it literally pour out of her and be soaked up by Kelley.

After a couple of minutes, she felt almost fine.

She leaned back towards he middle of the bed, her hair had become stuck to strands of red, which pulled wetly apart. Grabbing a fistful of tissues from the bedside cabinet she wiped her cheek and blew her nose.

Kelley didn't say anything for a moment; she nodded like they were sharing a revelation.

"A little better?" she offered.

Emily sniffed and dropped the balled-up wad of tissues onto the bed table. "Yes. Much better, thanks." She took a moment to compose herself, "and no, I think I'm going to be alright. I need to be stronger."

"Okay, but remember, we can always talk, yeah?"

A nod, "Yeah."

"Look, I'm sorry you had to hear all that from next door last night," Kelley slid the plastic chair back and sat.

"How – were you there too?"

"No. No, I spoke with the duty nurse earlier when I arrived. That can't have been pleasant."

"What Happened?" Emily asked, eagerly.

"Well, you'll know the lad died of course." She leaned in and lowered her voice, "Just don't let anyone know I talked about it, I'll be in huge trouble."

Emily shook her head quickly, "I won't."

"Okay, well the strangest thing. The guy seems to have been stabbed in the neck by his girlfriend late the previous night." She paused for a moment to glance at Little Mads lying on top of the blanket, "The doctors just about managed to save his life. But last night, somehow he must have woken up from his sedation and torn off the dressings. The neck wound opened up and he blead to death before they could do anything about it."

Emily's mouth hung open, "Shit." she began, "That's nasty. Was he from around here?"

"Yeah, local lad. Name of Ryan Mason."

Time seemed to stop. That name. It cut through Emily like an icy blade. That appalling git, that loser who had ruined her childhood.

He deserved to be dead, dead and gone.

There was a small plop sound and Emily was brought back from her furious thoughts.

"I'll get it." Kelley trotted round to the other side of the bed and collected Little Mads from the floor. She turned it over in her hands, feeling the fabric, looking into its glassy black eye. "You're a restless one, aren't you? Where were you going?"

Funny, Emily almost expected Little Mads, full of nothing but beans and fluff to answer her back.

It was cold in the flat. A couple of days unattended and it already was starting to smell a little damp.

Emily busied herself in the kitchen making a cup of tea while the little electric radiator in the living room worked its best to dispel the deep winter chill.

The fridge was still fairly well stocked with a few goodies that she and Mads were planning to share over Christmas and Emily was thankful that the milk was still good as she sloshed it into her tea.

The time wasn't much past lunch time, but the heavy grey clouds already cast a gloom over the day. It wasn't really going to get any brighter now. Emily craned her neck up through the kitchen window to see the sky between the tower blocks and wondered whether it might snow.

The living room had begun to warm a little, so Emily turned the thermostat knob on the radiator down slowly until it clicked. There wasn't very much money to keep the place any warmer than this.

She sat slowly in the middle of the couch and looked at her own face reflecting indistinctly in the TV screen.

She couldn't ever remember it being so quiet; there was usually some kind of commotion going on nearby. Noticing her bag on the coffee table, she unclipped Little Mads from the chain where it usually hung and propped it up in front of her on the table.

The little black eyes stared blankly back at her.

"Well, it's just you and me then I guess." The sound of her own voice in the silence startled her a little.

"You're all I have left of her." Unblinking beads regarded her coldly.

"I don't even know if I'll be allowed to live here. What will I do, where will I go?" She wasn't panicking just yet, but these were things that she was going to have to deal with soon.

"I mean, okay the flat's all paid for. It was Mads' Dad's place and he left it to her when he died." She took a sip of her tea, holding the mug to keep her hands warm. "But, well *legally*, I don't have any right to the place. Do I?" There was of course no answer.

"I mean, I guess I could just about pay the bills if I get a job. It won't be as bad as some people – they've got rent to pay." She sighed and wandered over to the window and stared down at the street below. It was empty.

"Maybe I should just pack it all in and go live with Mum and Dad again." She spun around, suddenly angry, "No! No, they abandoned me, they didn't lift a finger before when I came out to them." She stepped over to the table and picked up Little Mads and held her tightly, breathing in her faint coffee aroma.

"No," she repeated, quietly, "It's just you and me now."

CHAPTER 7

THE AFTERNOON HAD drawn into evening before
Emily really noticed the time. She had simply sat on
the couch trying not to think about her situation, and
so her mind had wandered here and there. For a while,
she had tried to recall happy moments when she was
a child, but it was like dredging grey, lifeless waters.

For a short while, she fantasised about a future life
with Mads where everything was perfect – they had
a lovely house, a dog even. The sun was shining and
they were laughing.

She found herself smiling through tears that ran
down her cheeks and turned cold in the chilly room.
They would have had a lovely future.

She needed to pee. What was more, she needed to

eat.

The first urgency dealt with Emily felt an icy chill as she crossed the living room to the kitchen. She was about to adjust the radiator when a low moan span her around to stare wide-eyed towards the window.

Another gust of wintery wind blew a sprinkling of fine snow crystals through a gap where the window was slightly ajar.

"Shit," she muttered, pulling the window closed, frustrated at the loss of cripplingly expensive heat. "Did I leave it open all this time?"

She made a point of pulling the handle firmly to the closed position and gave it a tug to be doubly sure.

This side of the block was all windows, so only Spiderman or Tom Cruise would have posed any credible threat to her at this height.

Snow though. She hoped it would settle, perhaps add a little beauty to the depressing landscape.

It was dark in the living room; only the light from the hallway spilling into the room casting a cosy glow. Outside, the tiny fakes swirled and swept through the air, lit from below by the streetlights.

The fancy turkey and ham pie in the fridge beckoned. This, plus pickles, cheese and crackers was to be the highlight of their boxing day fare. Emily had always preferred boxing day leftovers to the actual Christmas meal. Mads had relented to her pestering (including a couple of 'bed-time treats' as the clincher) and returned from her last shift before Christmas with bags laden with her favourites. The staff discount was a real life-saver, but they were close to broke now.

Mindful of that, Emily turned off the hallway light

and padded across the living room, muscle memory guiding her to the kitchen in the darkness. The tube-light plinked and flickered to life, causing her to squint for a short while.

After a couple of minutes, Emily emerged from the kitchen with a plateful of pie, cheese, pickles. The other hand, a cold can of cider. For now, she would eat like a queen, to waste it would be— what was that on the coffee table?

She halted at the sight of an unexpected shadow. She hadn't left anything there, not her bag, a pillow.

It shifted.

It was alive, a cat? Did a cat get in? There! A tail, now an ear—

"Where's that poppet of yours?"

Ice coursed through Emily's veins, her breath became cold stone in her chest.

The thing moved, unfolded in the blackness with a sound that Emily couldn't fathom. It was like something hard and heavy being dragged across the table.

"My?" Emily hadn't understood what the... the thing on the table had said, but her clumsy half-query was all the fearful questions that were clamouring for attention inside her head at once.

What *was* it? It wasn't a person, but it spoke. Her eyes were beginning to adjust to the blackness in the living room – were there wings? A part of herself felt relief, clutching at explanations, it was just a crow. It got in through the window.

"Hey! Shoo!" she attempted, placing her supper on the desk by the window. If she could open it back up again, maybe it would fly out.

"You can't dismiss me that way, I'm not a pestilent raven." This wasn't the voice of any bird. It was low, growling, slow and deliberate.

A million terrifying images flashed through Emily's mind. This wasn't anything normal or natural. Was it a demon, some nightmare creature that lurked in the darkness? What was it going to do, tear her apart? Drag her down into hell – both?

She began to weep with terror, it was between her and the door, blocking her escape. Stupid!

"Leave me alone! Please, just leave me alone," she pleaded.

"I'm not here to hurt you." Came the voice again. It shifted as if to move towards her.

"Stop! Keep back!" It froze, she was sure that its eyes were boring into her from the shadow. But it had stopped, there was a chance.

"Move over into the light so I can see you." She pointed a trembling finger to the patch of light spilling out from the kitchen.

Immediately, it hopped down between the table and the couch with a heavy thud. It was lost from her sight now and a surge of panic swept through her.

That feeling didn't subside when what looked like an enormous bat crawled out from the front of the couch and ambled into the pool of light.

Emily put her hand to her mouth to stifle a horrified gasp. The creature was the size of a very large cat, a sort of sandy brown colour. Behind it, stubby wings flexed as it settled its pot-bellied form onto the floor. It looked up at her with a grotesque face, half human but with those recurring bat-features cropping up again in its ears and snout.

The creature grunted, and scratched at its backside revealing a short thick tail tipped with what might have been an arrowhead.

My God, Emily thought, *I know what you are*.

"You're a gargoyle?"

"Yes Ma'am." It feigned a tug of imaginary forelock and grinned wickedly pointy teeth. "At your service."

"At *my* service?"

"I'm all yours," It scratched at its crudely displayed genitals, "If you'll have me."

Emily had taken the opportunity to sidle a little towards the desk and now had her hand on an antique glass paperweight. In a flash she hefted it at the gargoyle hitting it squarely on the forehead. The paperweight shattered and a cloud of dust and pieces of stone skittered across the floor.

The gargoyle rocked once and fell backwards onto the floor with a thump.

Elated, Emily rushed to inspect the defeated demon – Buffy could kiss her arse!

But before she reached the body, she was stopped by a wheezing cackle. The gargoyle pulled itself up into a sitting position and continued laughing. There was a definite crater in its forehead and as she watched, the stone shifted and moved to smooth over the wound.

"That was quite a pitch, young lady. I congratulate you. But please, I beg you no more." It reached around and gathered up a handful of fragments of stone and a few bits of glass then pressed them into its side where they seemed to be absorbed. The glass fragments winked in the light briefly before being sucked below the surface. "Listen carefully. I'm not here to hurt you. I'm here to help you. You *and* your beloved."

What the hell? Emily thought, *This thing is like that cop robot from the Terminator movies, how could it just heal itself like that?*

"I don't understand." She crouched down to get a better look at it. She didn't trust it, but she guessed that if it really was going to tear her apart and drag her screaming into the pits of hell it would have done so by now and there was probably nothing she could do about it.

"Your Lemman. The pale negress that your heart and loins throb for." He leered up at her, "I saw it happen. I was there."

Emily gasped, "You saw her die!"

"No." He sat upright, primly almost, wings folded flat against his back, tail coiled around with the tip in his lap, "I saved her from the hereafter."

"That's not true. The doctors say she never came round from the lightning strike in the alleyway."

He scoffed, "No simple thunderbolt. For sure, not a spear from God. I ask you now, fetch me your poppet."

Poppet? What did he mean? Suddenly it dawned on her. He meant Little Mads. What on earth did he want with that?

Well, there was no harm in finding out.

"You stay there, don't move." Emily got to her feet and backed up towards the bedroom, grabbed her bag and hurried back. She was expecting the thing to be gone or even leap out at her from the shadows, but there he was, sitting in the light just as she had left him.

She turned on a lamp and sat on the couch with her bag on the table.

"Okay, gargoyle, you can come over."

Without a sound, the impish creature bound over and sat obediently at the end of the table. It rocked a little under his weight at first.

She shook her head. *This was nuts.* But she unclipped the little cloth doll from her bag, which she shoved onto the floor then placed Little Mads in the middle of the table.

It was an old table; another of the antiques that Mads' dad had picked up from somewhere. It was solid, dark wood. The scratches and nicks in the surface would have told a hundred stories.

"I can smell her from here," the gargoyle muttered.

"That's the coffee beans." Emily replied.

"No." He leaned a little closer to get a good look, "She's inside, and she's still strong."

"What are you talking about?" Emily snatched up Little Mads and held her to her chest. "Just tell me what's going on, what the hell are you and what do you want?"

The gargoyle shuffled to the middle of the table and sat cross-legged in front of Emily. He looked up with stone eyes and appeared to take a long breath.

"My name is Gabriel. I'm quite ancient, where I come from is of no concern. I was conceived by magic, by whom you will have no care." He paused to let this sink in, but those basics were self-evident.

"The old woman you crossed. A witch by the name of Juliana, she was my mistress, but my employ is now at an end with her."

"She's the one that attacked us, SHE killed Mads!"

"Not so simple. But hold that truth in your heart for now. Know this though. When your sweet mulling lay dying, I saw her spirit ready to pass.

"It took near the last of my power to capture her light and place it into the poppet that you hold just as dearly. It makes a fine vessel for her soul; it was stitched with such fondness and your own heart holds it firm."

Emily's head was swimming. Mads was still alive? Her soul was *inside Little Mads?*

"But what's the point of being trapped inside here?" she held the doll up, "It's just cloth and beans and fluff, she can't move or talk to me."

Gabriel grinned widely and chortled, "Oh, Ho but she *does* move and live, and what wicked deeds she has done for you already at your command." He shook his head and laughed, "Did she not dispatch your childhood tormentor?"

"Ryan? No, he was stabbed by his girlfriend, probably something drug-related."

"Did she now?" Gabriel tilted his head, bat-like ears apoint, "And did his beloved come to him again in the night at the infirmaria? Did she walk like a spirit past all there to send him to his final sleep?"

"No... the news said she was arrested. So, you're saying Mads' ghost just floated out all by itself and killed Ryan?"

"Her spirit is held firm. She has a new body now,

and like a miting, she is learning to master it. And so she does for now under your command."

"I did no such thing! Besides, Ryan must have been attacked while I was asleep."

Gabriel lowered his head, his ears fell, "Perhaps through a window I crept that night, and perhaps a whisper in your ear while you slumbered." He looked up earnestly, "But only a suggestion. Just a thought for you to consider. The act was by *your* will alone, your psyche it was that reached out to your joy and pulled the strings that animated her to your bidding."

Emily looked at Little Mads; she was limp and lifeless. But then she remembered how she thought that it squirmed a little when they passed Ryan's room... and yes, how had it ended up on the floor.

She dared to hope that what Gabriel was trying to tell her in his funny way of speaking was true.

"She's alive? She can move?"

"She can. But by her own motivation, not for now. She must learn, and you must teach. For a time, she is nought but a golem."

The little stone imp, leapt to the side as Emily placed Little Mads onto the table in front of her.

"Show me," she said with determination.

"You have power within you, but it is weak. It concentrates while you sleep, but in wakefulness your mind is too concerned with the things of the day." He paused as if to consider something, "But there can be a way. I am a thing of magic and I know its ways. I can become a channel for you to increase your power."

"Okay, that sounds good... I think." Then warily,

"But why would you do that? What's in it for you?"

"We both would have the thing that we most desire. You would have your dear one, and I would have my life."

She looked at him quizzically.

"My life is ebbing away," he began, "The moment I broke service from the witch, my life began to wain. To survive, I must be bound to a master – or mistress, one with the power. You have the power within you. It is only a spark, but that ember can be kindled.

"Then, with that power, you can restore your precious."

"Okay." It all sounded decidedly dodgy, but if she could have Mads back then she really would sell her soul to the devil. "What do I need to do?"

"Just command me to your service." He sat neatly again.

"But how? I don't know any magic, or spells or anything."

"Just command me. Your heart knows your intent. Believe what you say and it will happen."

Emily cleared her throat; she felt a little silly but she thought about how much she wanted to be with Mads again. "Gabriel, gargoyle. I command you into my service," she intoned as grandly as she could manage.

At first, she thought it hadn't worked, then a tiny twinkling of golden specks danced briefly between them and was gone.

It was a little anticlimactic. If she were to be honest, she was expecting her hair to be blown about by a magical wind at least.

"Was that it?" she asked.

"Yes, mistress." Gabriel bobbed his head in deference.

"How do I know you're not joking?"

The gargoyle – now, officially her familiar looked hurt. "It's a sacred bond," he said solemnly, "Only you can undo it."

"So, you say I have magic powers or something? How come I didn't know about this?"

Gabriel thought for a moment, "It doesn't always show. Some carry the gift to their grave with not even a spark between their fingers."

"That's a terrible waste."

"But for most, the gift is like a seed that has gone to rot – just a tiny, withered thing." He looked up at her sadly, "The gift is very weak in you mistress."

Emily's shoulders sagged, "Oh. That's a bummer."

"We can nurture the gift." Gabriel said, hopefully, "Remember, I am born of old, powerful magic."

"Oh, that's fantastic!" She reached out without thinking to grab Gabriel by the cheeks but he backed off and nearly toppled off the table. "Does that mean," she continued, "that we can magic her back a body?"

"No. Well, this would be the work of a master sorcerer. We must bide our time and do what we can do."

"... And what's that then?" Emily was a little frustrated. She didn't really think that magic had such limitations.

"We'll make her live, under her own will within this vessel. You will have your joy back... In a sense."

"Okay. That sounds like a good start," she conceded. "How?"

"Now that we are bonded, you can be the conduit for a part of my power. It will flow from you, and soon your own power will grow. Place your poppet here, between us."

Emily carefully sat Little Mads in front of her on the table and looked at the gargoyle expectantly.

"What now? Do I need some kind of magic spell or words?"

"No," he scoffed, "Magic incantations are a falsehood, a fiction from tall tales and make-believe. The power you control has no words; it is a thing of the heart. You have no need of spells or bubbling potions to move your legs to walk nor wave a wand or stamp a staff to shit." He looked her in the eye with a knowing look and lowered his voice again, "You saw that when you commanded me into service, maybe even before some time."

He was right! Those words that she said when she bonded Gabriel were just some random bullshit. And yes, she HAD used her power before, she remembered the wild wind in the sanctuary, setting off the sprinklers at school and then the blast that seemed to come from her in the alley. That was the most powerful, one – and now that she recognised what it was, it made a little sense. It happened on its own when she thought Mads was in danger.

She nodded slowly, "I see what you're saying." She looked at the inert cloth doll on the table, sitting slightly lop-sided and wished – yes *wished* seemed to be the right word for it – for her to be alive.

Something like static prickled at the back of her head for a moment and Little Mads toppled over.

Gabriel sat watching intently, glancing from the doll to Emily, "That's it, keep going."

Again, Emily let all the hope in her heart pour out towards the slumped figure on the table. This time, the prickle became a warmth around her. Somehow this felt *right*, and she latched on to that feeling, letting it sustain and grow.

Little Mads twitched and flopped over.

It was only a tiny movement but it shocked Emily so much she cried out and the feeling of power instantly vanished. The room felt suddenly cold and dark.

"Did you see that!" Emily shouted, beaming. "She moved, she really moved all by herself."

"Look closer," Gabriel suggested.

Emily leaned in; Little mads had fallen onto her back, arms stretched out. She seemed just the same as usual. Emily squinted and moved a little closer.

"*Shit,*" she said under her breath, "She's breathing." Almost imperceptibly, the chest of the little doll was slowly moving in and out.

"Not in actuality," Gabriel said quietly, also with his nose just a few inches away from the figure, "It's just that she *thinks* that's what she ought to be doing. She's remembering what it is to be alive." He sat back with a satisfied look on his face, "And the body has awakened. Ready for your bidding again."

"My bidding, she's not my slave."

"For now, you have to be the mistress to us both. Your joy is still not fully awake. She drifts in a half-sleep, not yet aware. But that will come."

"So, she's definitely still in there?" Emily asked, looking into the small black eyes.

"Yes. Practice some more, the vessel needs exercise, your Joy can see and watch and learn. Just will it."

"Okay, I'll try to get her to stand." She leaned forward again on the couch and felt for the warm feeling she had experienced before.

Stand up, my love, show me that you're in there.

Straight away, Little Mads began to squirm. At first the movement looked unnatural and uncoordinated, then she pulled herself to a sitting position and then unsteadily up to her feet where she rocked slightly, seemingly panting with the effort.

Emily clapped her hands with joy and would have tried to hug Gabriel except she figured he wasn't the touchy-feely sort after last time.

"Oh, Gabriel, this is incredible. It's really true." She turned to Little Mads, "Mads, Mads! It's me, it's going to be alright." The doll stood, swaying slightly. No reaction.

"Remember, she can't act for herself yet, but no doubt she will see you, like in a dream." He hopped off the table and onto the arm of the couch to Emily's right. "You are doing well. Now something more of a task. Help her to think."

Emily looked about herself, what would she have her do? She looked back to the kitchen and saw the can she had dropped earlier. A little smile came to her face.

"Madeline dearest, do you think you could be an absolute darling and bring me a cider? There's one on the kitchen floor."

Without a moment of hesitation, Little Mads marched to the edge of the table and fell directly off the edge flat onto her face.

Gabriel burst into raucous laughter and almost toppled to the carpet himself. Emily held back a snort and lifted little Mads to her feet whereupon she marched resolutely towards the kitchen.

"That can's almost as tall as her, do you think she'll be able to lift it?" Emily asked.

"Oh, a golem can be as strong as a hundred their size. They have been used for thousands of years to do their masters' – uh, sorry and mistress' bidding."

Little Mads reached the dropped can and seemed to be examining it for a few seconds. Then she got behind it and started rolling it back to the living room.

Gabriel grunted, impressed, "The golem is also a crafty and resourceful tool."

The can rolled across the carpet with Little Mads behind it. It bumped into her ankle and came to a rest. She stopped, mission accomplished.

Emily let out a little giggle, "Thanks Mads." She lifted the waiting golem up on to the table where it continued to stand, unblinking black eyes looking into the space between them.

"Mads," she said quietly to the doll, "How are you doing in there? Can you hear me in there?"

Nothing.

It just stood on the table, pretending to breathe, waiting for the next command.

"Excellent." Gabriel said quietly. "Your ability comes naturally to you." He climbed down onto the floor and stretched with a soft grinding sound. His wings extended fully outwards, just a little further than his arms reached, then folded back neatly. He made a little satisfied sigh and hopped back onto the table where he curled up like a bloated cat.

"You will make an acceptable mistress," he said lazily.

For the next half hour, Emily experimented with some basic tricks, putting Little Mads through her paces – hopping on one foot, jumping, even at one point managing to leap from the back of the couch onto the coffee table. Mads had been fascinated by videos of urban parkour athletes on YouTube. She'd never had the courage to try it and Emily had been thankful for that.

A little later, Emily lay on the couch with Little Mads on her chest, just looking up at her bead-eyes. She reached over to the coffee table for her can and drained the last of it then looked over to where the gargoyle appeared to be sleeping.

"Gabriel, you pretend to breathe don't you."

He raised his head a little, "Yes. I don't need to of course but over the centuries it's become something of a habit."

"Wow, so old? Were you once a person then?"

"Oh no. I'm purely elemental. No human soul resides in this stone."

"So, what, you're just a lump of granite brought to life?" she asked.

The gargoyle sat bolt upright, chest puffed out indignantly, wings outstretched. "Madam! I am no common granite!" he bristled, "I am purest Cotswold limestone. The product of the lives of billions of creatures that swam in the ocean before your ancestors even cowered in filthy underground burrows!"

Oh, crap! Thought Emily, *I've racially offended a rock.*

"Uh, sorry. I didn't mean to upset you – I didn't know."

"I didn't *ask* for this form. This is how I was carved, and so it is that I am."

Emily sighed. It was getting a little late and she was tired.

"Look, I'm going to go take a shower then to bed. We can carry on with Mads in the morning." She got up and started towards the bathroom, "Will you be okay by yourself?" she turned to ask. He was standing on the table, watching her.

"Fifty million years of solitude under a hill was nothing to me." He scratched himself crudely and waved her on.

The water was bloody freezing as usual. Emily pushed open the glass folding door to the shower and grabbed her towel from the rail. As she shivered and dried herself off, she felt something underfoot.

"Ugh, what's that?" She lifted her foot from what looked like a couple of short trails of sand. Were had that come from?

She looked up to see if the ceiling was crumbling. Nothing more than a little flaking paint up there.

Never mind, she'd sweep it up in the morning.

She pulled on her pyjamas which were neatly folded on the washing basket and padded out to the living room.

Gabriel was curled up in the armchair in the corner of the room. Not asleep, but eyeing her as she walked in.

Little Mads was sitting on the coffee table where she left her.

"Do you sleep?" she asked Gabriel, stooping to pick up Little Mads.

"No." came the gruff reply. "I am cursed with eternal wakefulness. Go. Slumber, child. We have work in the morning."

CHAPTER 8

Now THAT SHE was home and in her own bed, it felt deeply unnatural to wake up alone.

Emily opened her eyes and realised that Little Mads was laying on her chest. She had put her on the pillow beside her where Mads used to sleep before drifting off. She smiled. It meant that she must have climbed up there by herself last night.

"Good morning Mads," she spoke softly, realising only after she had said it that she left the '*little*' off.

Little Mads shifted very slightly.

"That's it, find a way to push through," she said, picking her up.

Somehow, she seemed a little firmer, less like a bag of loose beans, more *coherent*. Emily hugged Little

Mads to her cheek and breathed deeply. She still smelled wonderfully of coffee.

Gabriel was still sitting on the chair where she'd left him last night, rigid and unmoving like the statue he clearly was.

Emily coughed, hoping to get his attention. With a grinding sound, he began to move, stretching his wings and arms. "You're up then?" he said snarkily, idly scratching his privates.

"You WERE asleep!" Emily laughed.

"Tickle-brained Tewkesbury mustard! I was not!" He scowled and hopped onto the arm of the couch with his tail wrapped around in front of himself. "Sleeping is for you offal-bags," he muttered.

"Tickle-what? Oh, never mind. I'm getting breakfast."

A mince pie, crackers, cheese, another hunk of turkey and ham pie. That was always going to have been Emily's Between Christmas and New Year breakfasts. She'd not quite degenerated to the point of washing it down with a tin of cider, though she did think that a little alcohol might take the edge off the weirdness that had invaded her life.

Gabriel watched her eat while a crappy Christmas movie played out on TV.

"That boy who died?" Gabriel suddenly asked, "How do you feel about that?"

Emily bit into a cheese-laden cracker and Little Mads watched the crumbs fall back onto the plate. "Not gonna lose a lot of sleep over him," she said after swallowing.

"So you're glad?"

"I don't think he deserved to *die*, no. But he *was* a total scumbag. Him and his mates. They pretty much ruined our lives."

The gargoyle nodded silently.

"But you knew that though, didn't you?" She looked at him suspiciously. "How?"

He scratched at the patch of moss on his chin, "All my life, I've been watching people. I'm good at it. For hundreds of years, hanging from my church seeing folk flock to grovel before their maker, mourn their dead, join themselves to their betrothed." He shuffled to look her right in the eye, "I see the little things that people do and how they feel. So yes, I could tell from peering through the windows how you felt about that boy."

"You were spying on me in the hospital."

"Watching. Yes."

"Hmmm." She bit into the delicious crust of her pie and chewed. "Why?"

"So I could know how to serve you," he said primly.

"You were so sure I'd agree then?"

"You have been wronged. The others you mentioned. They must be punished—"

"No more deaths." Emily said firmly, "They're out of my life now, so they can just rot. I've seen them, they haven't amounted to anything. Let them fester."

"But mistress," he cooed, "Nor have you. Your life is as simple as theirs, they took away your potential, your love... even your future."

"I have Mads here. When she's better, we can carry on," she said defiantly.

"But wouldn't it delight you to scare them. To

give to them a taste of your misery?" He looked to Little Mads who now appeared to be listening to the conversation, "A little retribution won't hurt. Will it? Now that you have the means." He reached out a talloned finger and gently stroked Little Mads' cheek. "This is just the kind of work that the golem is meant for. To exact revenge, do dirty deeds."

She looked towards Little Mads, who turned her head back to look right back at her.

Gabriel grinned, wickedly sharp teeth. "Your poppet agrees, yes?"

She sighed. It *would* be nice to teach them a lesson, to freak them out a bit.

"Can we be sure that nobody gets hurt? Especially Mads."

"We can but try. It will be good for your poppet too."

"Okay then," she relented. "What do you suggest?"

"Oh!" He clapped his hands, it made Little Mads jump, "The fun we shall have. What say we conjure a haunting. Have these scoundrels swear that they are being visited by the spirit of your departed sweeting. Send your golem to steal into their houses and make quiet mischief while they rest."

Now, that *did* sound like fun, "Can we do that? How?"

"My dear mistress, the best is to be laid before you like a king's feast." He shuffled closer. "*Farsight*," he said conspiratorially.

"Far–?"

"She has the facsimile of eyes stitched into her head. So, the power you hold makes those glassy adornments more than eyes of flesh. Those eyes, bound to you by your power can give you the sight that your beloved witnesses."

"I can do *that*? Show me!"

"The truth of it is that you only need to think it," he said simply. "Just close your eyes."

Emily did as she was told then imagined that she could see what Little Mads was seeing.

At first, all she could see was the brownish orange inside her eyelids, then a face was looming down at her – her own face! She shrieked in delight and surprise, but in doing so opened her eyes and the vision collapsed.

"Oh," she said, still beaming, "I need to keep my eyes closed. It's also hard when there's still light." She thought for a moment then darted off to the bedroom.

A few seconds later, she came back with a thick black scarf. "Mads bought me this last Christmas," she said cheerily.

Gabriel scoffed disinterestedly, but watched her nonetheless as she wrapped the scarf around her head and tied it in a loose knot at the back. She then positioned the improvised blindfold over her eyes and began again.

"Ha! This is much better," she said moving her head about. Little Mads' head turned in unison with hers, then the little cloth golem held her hand up to her face and waggled it about.

"Whoah," she gasped, "I've always wanted to try that VR thing. Now I've got my own real-life one." She giggled and sent Little Mads to the edge of the coffee table. She wobbled a little on the edge of the couch, not used to the relative height.

Emily pulled herself towards the back of the couch, crossed her legs and felt about for the cushions to either side. She jammed them up against herself for stability and then launched Little Mads off the edge of the table and across the room. She did a lap at a fast jog, under the table then climbed the leg, up on top and leapt for the back of the couch. She ran along the back of it full pelt then leapt into the void off the end and just made it, scrambling onto the edge of the desk by the window.

From there, she climbed the curtains and shuffled along the curtain rail. She paused for a moment to look down – her heart was pounding with exhilaration. Then, she had an idea.

"Gabriel, catch me!" She launched Little Mads off the rail into the air towards the couch. In a flash, the stone monstrosity hurled himself across the room with a thump and deftly caught her in what seemed like a gigantic, clawed hand. As he ambled back to the couch, Emily felt a little like Fey Wrey in the clutches of King Kong.

He carefully allowed the doll to climb out of his hand and stand panting gently on the table.

Emily tore the scarf off and whooped. "That was fucking amazing! How the hell did I – we? Do that?"

"As I said," the gargoyle intoned flatly, "You only need to think it to make it happen. Do you *see* what the power can do now?"

"She's thinking for herself too isn't she?"

"Yes." He turned to look at the still panting figure on the table, "Quite impressive progress."

"What about night vision?"

Gabriel looked at her askance.

"We need to send Mads out late at night, don't we? Am I going to be able to see in the dark?"

Gabriel flicked his wrist nonchalantly, "Go. Try it. I wager you know the answer already."

Emily shrugged and pulled the scarf back over her eyes.

Little Mads hopped off the table again and into the little corridor towards the bedroom and bathroom. It was a little gloomy in there but she saw well enough.

Under the bed was a lot darker, especially as the curtains were still drawn. And yet, she could see just as well. *This is going to work*, she thought.

Then it occurred to her.

"Only one problem," she said. "I don't know where Ian lives."

Gabriel shrugged, "Don't look at me, I'm just a gargoyle not a genie."

"Hang on, I'll see if I can find him online." She wandered over to the desk and opened up their laptop. The girls both shared a beaten up, refurbished wreck but it was good enough for what they needed it for.

The laptop *was* old, and it was slow too. Tired of waiting for it to start up, Emily busied herself in the kitchen making a cup of coffee. A glob – a *generous* glob – of brandy cream stirred in made it just a little *festive*.

When she got back, the desktop was finally starting to populate with icons, the hard-drive thrashing away with furious insect chittering.

Her coffee was beginning to warm her by the time

she had a browser window open.

In a couple of minutes she had found a respectable looking website that allowed her to look up Ian's name and location.

"Got it!" she exclaimed. "Look, there's only one Ian Thompson in this area."

Gabriel climbed up onto the desk to get a better look at the screen.

"Ok, so click on his name, let's see where this pustule lays his head."

Emily turned to look at Gabriel, "Huh? How come you know what to do? I'd have thought you'd be screaming about witchcraft or something."

"You're a fine one to be talking about witchcraft missy," he said calmly. "Besides, my previous master – before my gladly departed witch-mistress, he used to prod and fawn over one of these magic mirrors day and night."

"Hm. Surprises upon surprises, a tech-savvy gargoyle... Ah! Dammit."

Emily had clicked on the link to view the address, but the website was asking for registration and payment for the privilege.

"One must always grease the palms of a good snitch." Gabriel cackled.

Their bank account was all-but empty. Fifteen pounds wasn't a great amount, and the site offered up to six full records for the price. She could hunt down the rest of the gang.

But she had no income, now no way to – wait, didn't Kelley say she would pay for helping with her research?

She brightened.

"Okay, screw it let's do it," she said through gritted teeth as she started filling in the registration form. Her finger paused over the mouse-button for a moment, then clicked the golden PayPal PAY button and it was done.

"Holy shit!" she gasped, "Look! He lives in one of the tower blocks on our estate!"

Indeed, the boy, now grown who had caused the girls so much anguish had been living not five minutes walk from them for all these years.

The electoral role records showed that he'd lived alone there for two years.

"I know the place too," Gabriel sneered, "I had dark business in that tower not a dozen days ago." He looked up at Emily, the light from the laptop casting sinister shadows on his face, "We've caught the pestilent poke-buttock."

It seemed like a good idea to sleep early and set her alarm for 3am, but when Emily's phone began to vibrate and chirp, she felt like it would have been better to have just stayed awake – or maybe not bother with this at all.

She turned over sleepily and swiped the screen to shut the infernal thing up.

Just before the light from her phone's screen shut off, she noticed Little Mads standing over it in the dark.

She flipped on the bedside light. There she was.

"Are you waiting?" she asked, "You want to teach Ian a lesson?"

Slowly, jerkily, her head bobbed down and back up again.

"Oh my God. Mads, you can hear me?"

Again, she nodded but it looked like the effort was causing her pain. Emily scooped the golem up in her arms and hugged her.

"Okay, then. Let's teach this... *poke-buttock* a lesson."

Gabriel was in his usual 'sleeping' position on the armchair, but this time he straightened as soon as Emily entered the room.

"Time?" he said, clambering across the room to the coffee table.

"Yes, time." The sleepiness had all but left her now with the excitement.

Gabriel quietly watched her pad into the kitchen and clatter about for a couple of minutes. She emerged with a large mug of 'festive' coffee and a mince pie. She had already stuffed half of it into her mouth by the time she sat in the couch.

Little Mads climbed up the leg of the table and sat between Emily and Gabriel, waiting.

"She can definitely hear me," she said, swallowing the mouthful of pie. "She nodded when I asked her a question."

"Good." The gargoyle looked down at the little figure on the table, "Excellent progress."

Little Mads turned back to look briefly at Gabriel, then back to Emily.

"See!" she breathed, "She's waking up."

Emily took a long gulp of the coffee, scoffed the remainder of the mince pie then made herself comfortable on the couch as before. She took a long breath and then wrapped the scarf around her head, blacking out the dimly lit room.

Straight away, she was able to see herself towering up above... no, not herself, Mads.

"Do you have a plan?" Gabriel asked.

"Yes," she replied craftily, "I thought about it before I slept. This is really going to freak him out." She paused. "Crap. Um, I can't get outside. Can you get the door?"

"As you command mistress." He grunted, lumbered over to the door and reached up for the latch.

Emily guided Little Mads over to the door and through the gap that her familiar had opened for her. The cold night air swept in, hungrily seeking out the warm corners of the room.

"Jeez, that's cold. Can you close it now?"

He did as he was told and took up his position on the table in front of her.

"Will you allow me to see?" he asked. "You only have to will it."

She nodded, and as naturally as breathing, allowed Gabriel to join her.

They both saw the walkway, lit sporadically by small fluorescent overhead lights. Looking up at the sky above the balcony, the city lights illuminated low snow-laden clouds giving a useful amount of background light.

"Okay," Emily said gritting her teeth, "Let's go."

And off she scampered, quick as a rat. Along the walkway to the stairwell, leaping down the steps and launching off the wall at the bottom, towards the next flight down. In no time at all, five floors downward and out into the parking space.

She stopped for a moment to orient. This way, two tower blocks down, eighth floor, flat number 809.

She ran. Effortless, faster than she had ever known. Something was seeping into her conciseness, was it from Mads? A feeling of the overwhelming joy of running.

In no time at all, they reached the end of the parking space below their block, across the path at the end and over the deserted road which ran between them and the next two blocks.

It was a direct, straight route. Onwards down the concrete canyon they powered until they were below Ian's block.

But there was a problem.

Two hooded figures sat in the entrance to the stairwell. They ducked back behind the wheel of a car to observe.

The orange light of a cigarette lit up the inside of one of the hoodies. Acne scarred face, a gap-toothed grin as he passed the joint to his friend and received the bottle the other was holding.

There was no way they could get past these two unseen.

Emily looked upwards. The building was festooned with satellite dishes, flags, Christmas lights all attached by residents in clear contradiction to the building regulations that at least *most* of *her* neighbours followed.

This was the rough side of the estate – no big surprise to find that this was where Ian lived.

But, she realised this could be to their advantage. The amount of junk hanging from the building might just make useful handholds for a tiny, lithe figure to climb up.

Little Mads leapt up on to the bonnet of the car with a soft thump.

The junkies in the doorway didn't notice.

Up onto the roof, then a leap... and catching onto a vast Jamaican flag hanging from the first-floor walkway. Climbing that was no challenge and they found themselves up on the concrete balcony wall.

A few steps over, a set of Christmas lights had partly fallen and were dangling down from the floor above. Tugging experimentally on the string of lights proved it to be safe to climb and quickly they were up onto floor number two.

That should do it. They could make the rest of the ascent by the stairs now. They were just—

A pair of gigantic green eyes flashed before Emily's vision, sharp white teeth and a paw bearing dagger-like claws swiped Little Mads off the ledge and into the void.

Emily screamed as they fell, tumbling towards the dirty concrete below. When they landed, Emily could almost *feel* the impact, it was like falling in a dream.

One of the junkies looked up at the sound of a soft thud of something falling from the sky near to them.

"Whas' that?" he slurred.

"Ha! F'kin pigeon. Must've flown into a winda'," he scoffed.

"I'm gunna boot it," the first one announced, rising unsteadily.

"Whu for?"

"Dont wan the stinkin' thing flappin' about if iss..." he paused to belch, "if iss, not dead."

The other made vague sounds of concurrence before swigging from the bottle.

The drunk reached the spot where Little Mads had landed and stooped down. He pulled back his hoodie and yelled – "S'gone!"

He circled about unsteadily, calling "Cooo, Cooo little f'kr where you gone."

Someone shouted from above about calling the police which earned them two middle fingers thrust in a general upwards direction, he wasn't sure where the complainant was.

"C'mon," he called to his companion, "Less, fuck off somewhere else."

After a few very convincing grumbles, the other limbered to his feet, turned back quickly to retrieve the bottle and joined his friend in the direction of the broken-down children's play area.

A pair of black, glittering eyes watched the pair stagger off across the parking area from beneath a car. The coast was clear.

Back at the flat, Emily let out the breath she had been holding in. She had completely panicked when the cat had swiped them off the ledge and froze when they landed face-up in the car park. It had only been Mads' quick thinking to pick herself up and dart quietly under the car that had saved the day.

Emily couldn't see him, but Gabriel was quietly grinning to himself.

"She's starting to react by herself now," the gargoyle

said smoothly.

"She sure is," Emily breathed, still rattled. "Thanks Mads."

A warm feeling came back to her over the aether and she knew she had been heard.

"Let's give this another go then," she muttered, adjusting the pillows to her sides.

The way up was straightforward, but Emily was glad that she couldn't smell from where she was. The stairwell was littered with trash and unspeakable things. Mads easily bounded up the steps, all eight floors, then stood motionless at the exit that lead on to the walkway outside the row of flats at that floor.

809. The last but one.

They made their way along the silent walkway, counting off the numbers on the doors to their right. One flat still had light streaming out from a window, sounds of gaming could be heard faintly from within. Pity the neighbours that lived next to this guy.

The dark blue and peeling paint of door number 809 rose above them. The window to the side was in darkness.

Despite being at least five times her height above her, Mads leapt to the letterbox, clung to the flap and gradually squeezed through.

She fell with a gentle plop onto the worn carpet on the other side.

The flat was in almost complete darkness, but Emily was impressed that she could make out her surroundings.

They were in a short, t-shaped corridor. A door at the end of it where it branched to the left and right was slightly jar.

Creeping past trainers and various tatty cardboard boxes they reached the junction.

To the left, snoring gave away Ian's bedroom, another door to its side likely a small store-room.

Emily had noticed on the way in that of the two windows to the right of the front door, one seemed to have been frosted.

The bathroom was as she expected, the first door on the right.

Ian was lazy; the door was also ajar. Mads pushed inside, hopped up onto the bath and walked along the edge towards the sink. The mirror above it was grubby, and a tube of toothpaste lay in the sink where it had been discarded.

With her foot, she squeezed a gob of paste onto a toothbrush. Standing on the back of the sink, Mads daubed a large letter 'M' on the mirror.

Emily considered rinsing the toothbrush off in the filthy toilet, but thought better of it. She didn't want to *kill* him. Somehow, she felt Mads didn't approve of her lenience.

She had to almost force Mads to drop the toothbrush in the sink and hop down onto the carpet – *God, who has carpet in the bathroom?* She thought.

The kitchen was at the end of the passage and had no door. The vinyl was slightly sticky underfoot and in the centre was a shabby dining table strewn with a few oddments and an empty ketchup bottle.

They climbed the leg and swept the bits and pieces to the edge of the table and leapt from there to the counter.

Reaching down, Little Mads opened up each of the drawers in turn. The cutlery drawer was pitiful, not what she needed. Then she spied three boxes at the end of the counter; new, unopened.

Bingo! Three boxes of steak-knives. Not a chance they were for his own use, likely robbed from a store hoping to be sold on.

The boxes were sealed pretty tightly, so a grubby butter knife was employed to tear open the seals. With the boxes emptied and the knives freed, the cloth golem took a deadly-sharp knife in each of its mitten-hands and leapt off the counter – and onto the kitchen table.

There, she laid the knives out and returned for two more. Back and forth she went until eighteen shiny knives lay in neat rows on the kitchen table.

She stood back to admire her work. Emily shuddered; this was creepy. Gabriel of course thought this was marvellous and cackled.

Suddenly Emily's farsight grew dim and the colour drained from her vision.

"Hasten, mistress!" the gargoyle cried, "She weakens. Bring her back to your bosom!"

Without a second's hesitation, Little Mads dropped off the table and scampered back round the hallway to the door where she leapt for the letterbox but missed and fell to the carpet. Emily's head began to swim as she felt Mads' energy draining.

She looked about and saw one of the boxes by the door. Leaning against it, she pushed it slowly towards the door, hopped up onto it and jumped for the letterbox. She scrabbled at the opening but found it hard to get a purchase on the flap, which hinged inwards.

Emily stopped, she was sweating profusely and tried again. This time, the flap opened enough to get a tiny arm behind and push it open. The golem squirmed through and dropped to the ground on the other side, letting the letterbox clang shut behind her.

It didn't matter anymore if Ian woke, she was out of the house, but their vision was starting to become grainy.

She staggered. No way on earth she could run down eight flights of steps.

A cold flush swept over Emily as they both realised the only way to get down in time.

She climbed up a bike propped against the balcony wall and stood on the edge, looking down into the depths below, swaying gently.

"Oh, crap." Emily muttered to herself, "This is too h—"

Mads jumped.

Arms outstretched, like a sky diver, the tiny figure fell from the building. It seemed to take forever, until the last moments when the ground suddenly rushed up to them and all became blackness.

Emily screamed. She waved her arms about in the darkness crying for Mads.

Slowly, the lovingly stitched doll turned over onto her back and Emily could see the moon and the streetlights again.

"Oh my God, Mads, you're okay. Thank fuck for that. Quick, let's get you home."

They got up onto their feet and ran back towards their

block. All the while, Emily's farsight grew dimmer and more indistinct. Little Mads was slowing down too. As they reached the road she slowed to a jog and stumbled. At the middle, Emily's vision completely disintegrated into grainy patches of grey and black which burst in her vision and vanished.

Emily tore off the scarf and swore.

"She's collapsed in the middle of the road!" she yelled hoarsely to the gargoyle.

Jumping up from the couch, she pounced on her boots and yanked her jacket from the hook by the door and fled, stifling a sob.

"I'm coming... I'm coming to get you," she breathed over and over as she ran helter-skelter down the stinking stairs and out into the car park.

With all the energy she could draw, she ran down the middle of the car park towards the end where the road crossed. A minute of agony and she was there, gasping and looking desperately around the road where she had last seen Mads trying to cross.

She had gone.

The freezing air bit into her now, turning the sweat on her neck and back to icy fingertips drawing down her skin.

Where was she? Tears started to sting at her eyes as the wind blew and tiny spiteful flakes of snow bit at her face.

The wind gusted again, and with it she thought it carried a voice. She turned, there was nobody there.

She strained to hear, but was only met by the ever-present sounds of the city.

Again. A sound, a mewling, like a small animal.

There! In the dying and damaged shrubbery between the car park and the path, sat a tiny shape, leaning forwards. It fell sideways.

"Mads!" Emily cried and was upon her in three bounds, sweeping her up and holding her tightly to her chest.

Her head lifted slowly and looked up.

"Thanks," she said.

CHAPTER 9

THE DOOR BURST open and Emily tumbled inside gasping for breath. Startled by the sudden noise, Gabriel crouched, defensively, tail arching over his back like a scorpion.

"She Spoke!" Was all that she could manage as she bent double, trying to slow her breathing. Then again, with a little more composure, "She's coming back to me. But she's so limp. Look, she's not moving!"

She kicked off her boots, flung her jacket over the hook and collapsed onto the couch, holding Little Mads to her chest.

The doll lay inert on her body, she felt loose inside.

"She needs to feed," Gabriel advised. "You have to do it now or she could perish."

"Feed? How?" She looked up at the stony face leering above her.

"She must draw on your power as a babe would suckle at your teat." He cackled and shambled over to the armchair in the corner of the room. "Don't worry. It will come naturally to you. You have a *feel* for the power now."

The stone monstrosity was right. So far, all she had needed to do was imagine herself using her power and it just... happened. Of course the trick was to know what it was that she could actually *do*.

Emily lay back on the couch and placed Little Mads on her chest, over her heart and thought... *nourishing* thoughts. Soon, a gentle golden glow began to form between them. She shifted her head and saw that there were faint filaments, along which pulses of light could be seen to gently flow.

It felt good. It felt warm and comforting. She guessed that was how a mother might feel nursing her child. She felt grateful for the opportunity to give her life-giving energy to another; bittersweet that she might never give life to a child of her own.

As she relaxed, she wondered when Kelley would call back with the results of her scan. Could she ever bear children?

Gently, the glow faded and stopped. The warm feeling drifted away like a dream and she felt the cold in the room. Of course it was nonsense to wonder about bearing a child. What was she thinking?

Little Mads stirred and sat up.

Gabriel grunted in approval and curled up on the armchair like a grotesque cat, watching.

"Hello you," she said sweetly to the little figure.

Little Mads tilted her head.

"I'm... I'm alive?"

"Yes! Yes, Mads you're alive." Emily choked, "Oh God it's unbelievable but it's really true."

She hugged the little figure tightly, Mads squirmed.

"It's been like I was in a dream," Mads said when her head popped out. "I dreamt crazy things, like I was watching myself from inside." She struggled out of Emily's arms and stood on her belly.

For a second or two, she looked about the flat, then lifted her arms, then legs to examine herself. Finally, she stood and looked Emily in eyes and addressed her, deadly serious. "What am I? What happened?"

Emily picked Mads up, placed her gently on the table and explained as best she could about the explosion in the alley, her time in hospital and the frightening incident with Ryan.

Mads sat in rapt attention, shaking her head slowly in astonishment at every revelation.

"This Gabriel. He's still here?" Mads asked when Emily needed to pause.

"I am bound to your Lemman." Came a voice from the armchair. Mads couldn't see it from there and she craned her neck to see who had spoken.

"Gabriel, would you come and introduce yourself to Mads?" Emily said over her shoulder.

With a grunt, the stone creature shuffled out of the chair and climbed up and onto the back of the couch. He looked down at Mads on the table, made a little bow then settled, perched behind Emily near her shoulder.

Mads looked up at Gabriel with fascination. "Oh. Emily said you were a gargoyle. Aren't you a grotesque? I couldn't help noticing—"

"The lack of a lead pipe up my arse?" He lifted his tail, if any proof were needed, "God's Hooks, she's bright. Yes, little one, my purpose was purely decorative." He settled back down. "But no matter, a common error to call me gargoyle. Besides," He stroked the soul-patch of moss on his chin, "The word *grotesque* has earned new meaning of late. It doesn't suit or serve me well."

Emily yawned, "I'm fit to drop now."

Mads climbed up into her lap, "Thank you for... I don't even know what it was... recharging me?" She thought for a moment. "Is this how it has to be from now? Do you have to keep feeding me? You're going to be dog-tired if you do.

"No." Gabriel interjected. "You can feed yourself. You can even feed Emily when she needs it."

The girls turned to look at Gabriel.

"Go sleep, you both. The dawn is long distant. You can learn tomorrow."

"He's right, you know," Emily mumbled sleepily, "I'm just about done." She pulled at her black t-shirt and grimaced, "I need another shower first. And you need a clean as well if you're coming to bed with me."

Mads looked up from Emily's lap. Slowly, the stitched mouth pulled itself into a semblance of a grin.

"Tomorrow, you will torment the other fools." Gabriel purred.

"We've gotta do that," Mads enthused, "I really wish I could see Ian's face when he sees all that creepy shit I did in his flat."

Emily picked Mads up and headed to the bathroom, "I'm not too sure. I nearly lost you this time, I can't lose you again Mads, I really can't."

Mads looked up from the sink where she had been carefully deposited.

"I'll be okay. Besides, we just didn't know that I needed my energy topping up." She paused to eye Emily as she stripped off, "You can give me another boost before I go out tomorrow."

"Scott then?" Emily dumped her clothes into the washing basket, "He's always been hanging around bloody Ian."

"Yes, Scott. I actually know where he lives. I saw his name on one of the delivery dockets from work."

"Smart! Where?"

"Same block as Ian! Two floors down," she announced triumphantly.

"Figures." Emily put the plug into the sink and ran some warm water in, about a third deep. She took a hand towel and placed it on the other side of the sink. "Your bath, madam," she said grandly.

Mads climbed gingerly in, and immediately the water began to turn a grey colour. "Shit, you really need that bath."

Emily stepped into the shower and turned on the water. "God knows where you went while I was in hospital," she called out.

Mads stopped cleaning herself for a moment, "That's a really frightening thought, you know. I mean I could have been *anywhere*." She carried on splashing water across her cloth body. It was starting to soak in, and she could feel herself getting heavy with water.

The plug pulled out of the sink with a '*blork*', and the dirty water drained away.

The shower stopped and Emily stepped out; her pale skin slightly pink from the hot water.

She grabbed a towel and wrapped it round her head, then noticed the sodden cloth doll standing in the sink, dripping.

Mads took a second to admire Emily's breasts. "You know," she began slightly wistfully, then looked down at herself "If I'd have known I'd end up this way, I might have sewn myself a decent cleavage. I know I wasn't exactly busty when I was... well, a human," she chortled, "But look at me now! Flat as a pancake!" Mads laughed and shook herself to get some of the water out of her.

"Oh, Mads. You know I always thought you were hot as hell. Those muscles were *such* a turn-on."

Mads climbed out of the sink and pulled the hand towel around herself, "Don't you go starting to get all horny now," she admonished, "I can't do an awful lot about it like this."

Emily sagged, in mock sadness and pulled the towel from her head to dry herself off.

"Unless..." Mads began, wryly.

"Hmmm?" came the sound from under the towel.

"Well," continued Mads, "There's always *Bruce*!"

The two girls erupted into peals of laughter at their own very private joke.

Emily picked Mads up and gave her an experimental squeeze. Just a couple of drops came out.

"I think it's the hair drier for you, girl," she smiled.

Scott's phone buzzed and blasted out some obscure drum-n-bass tune that he swore to everyone else was an unappreciated classic. As ringtones went, it was horrible, but as something that would wake a person after downing an entire two litre bottle of black-lightning the night before, it was entirely fit for purpose.

An arm flopped out of the bed, more by gravity than will and fumbled about for the offending slab. His fingers grasped it and pulled it back into the covers like some ghastly undersea creature drawing its prey back into a dark crack in the rocks.

"Bruv' I'm seriously freaking out." Came a voice from the phone. It was Ian, he certainly sounded scared.

"Seriously, mate. It's early." It wasn't. It was past ten. Scott sat up in bed; an empty can rolled out from a fold in the duvet onto the floor.

"I'm not jokin' Look, I've been broken into."

"You was robbed?" He rubbed an eye with the back of his hand. "Fuck."

"No bruv', someone got in and did some freaky shit in my flat." He paused, uncertainly, "though they didn't come in the door."

"How come?"

"There's a box and shit in front of the door. They coulda got *in* though the door, but not out with the box there."

"They take much? Aw, shit they didn't take my FIFA did they? I shouldn't have borrowed you it."

"No, least I don't *fink* they robbed nuffing."

"So, what then?"

"I told ya, they did freaky shit. Drew on my bathroom mirror, fuck man, they put all knives out on the table in neat little rows."

"Them posh steak knives?"

"All of them!" His voice rose to a squeak.

"Harsh." Scott breathed. Then, "You sure you not trippin'? Cos that blow you got the other day... Shit, that's rough as dog shit."

"I'm not trippin' bruh, I'm telling you the truth. Someone was in here but I can't figure out how. Or why."

Scott was just about waking up now and a cold realisation started to hit him like a slow-motion car crash.

"Oh, no no no. This ain't good," he mumbled. "Ian, mate it's rival dealers. They're tryin' to shut us down or scare us off or summink."

"Fuck that shit!" Ian was hopping from foot to foot now. "I told you, we oughta wait until J showed up again. That old-school crap is bad news."

"It *is* shit, but that's all that's out there now." Scott sighed, "I'd eat my grandma out for a hit on J's Purple Haze right now. You got a tube left?"

"Nah. Huffed my last one two days ago."

"Okay, look," Scott said carefully, "Let's just lay low for a couple of days. See what happens with J. She won't be gone for long. We've done okay since she went missing. Besides," he rationalised, "we're just small fish. There's gonna be some serious fuckers moving in on this manor soon and there's no way we want to get caught up in that."

There was a few seconds of silence on the line while Ian absorbed this.

"Alright. Makes sense," he conceded.

At around the same time that morning the girls were lounging on the couch watching a random cheesy Christmas movie.

Gabriel had retired to his armchair – his self-claimed spot now, it seemed – unimpressed with the TV show.

Emily's phone rang. She groaned and reached out to the coffee table to pick it up.

"It's Kelley!" she said excitedly. "My scan."

Mads scrambled onto the arm of the couch to listen. Over in his corner, Gabriel's large ears pricked up.

"Emily, Hi. It's Kelley Stranack – from the hospital. How are you getting on?"

"Oh, um not so bad. I think I've come to terms with things now," she said, looking over to Mads.

"That's great. It's not easy." She paused for a beat, "Anyhow. Guess you're interested to know the results of your scan?"

Emily could feel butterflies in her stomach, "Yes, kind of." She played it cool.

"Good. Do you think you can come into the hospital so that I can go over it with you? Nothing bad of course, but easier for you to be here." She paused again, as if she had something delicate to broach, "Maybe we can run another little test if you're willing?"

"Um, sure." At this point she would probably agree

to anything, just to get to finally hear once and for all what was going on inside herself.

"Lovely. Look, I know it's a little way to the hospital so I'd be able to book you a taxi on my research budget. Sound good?"

"Yeah, what time?"

"Just a sec." There was a muffled sound as Kelley put the phone down to check something, "How does one, this afternoon sound? It's really quiet here this time of the year. I'll grab some sandwiches from the canteen – any preference?"

And free lunch? This was sounding better and better, "Nope, anything. Surprise me!" She laughed awkwardly.

"Oh, there are some interesting surprises at the canteen. Catch you later then. Just come to the urology department."

Emily put the phone down and turned to Mads. "Wow. This is it then? I get to finally know what the hell I am."

"You'll always be my little chicken," Mads joked. "Honestly, whatever they found you'll always be you."

Relieved that the main entrance to the hospital had a covered drop-off area, Emily thanked the taxi driver, stepped out and grimaced at the rain pouring beyond.

Mads had insisted on coming along. She had the option to be stuffed inside Emily's rucksack or hang from the chain. She chose to hang so she could see what was going on, but keeping perfectly still might be a bit of a challenge.

"Okay, let's do this." Emily said as if to herself and headed inside.

The urology department was clearly marked on the big sign wall and turned out to be pretty easy to find – just down one short corridor off the big central spine that ran most of the length of the hospital.

Presumably, Christmas decorations had been deemed an infection hazard, but some smart-Alec had placed LED tealights inside four clear sample cups at reception and written the letters N-O-E-L on them with a sharpie. They flickered merrily away while Emily waited for someone to come to the desk.

A young Asian woman appeared from the office and gave her a friendly smile.

"Emily Moon, to see Kelley Stranack."

The receptionist tapped at her keyboard quickly, "Yes, Miss Moon, just take a seat for a moment, please." She indicated the small seating area and returned to her computer.

She had only just sat down when the door to one of the consulting rooms opened up and Kelley slid out. Emily noticed that she had changed her hair and now wore it in a magnificent bushy red ponytail. Was it really that long when she had met her last? She shook her head and stood to greet her.

"Hi Kelley, thanks for seeing me." Why was she feeling nervous all of a sudden?

"No, the pleasure is all mine," she said smoothly and beckoned her to follow back to the door she had just come from.

"Please, take a seat."

Emily hung her bag over the back of the chair, being

careful to ensure that Mads was dangling where she could probably see what was going on. Kelley passed her in the small room and sat behind the desk. That coconut shampoo again. Emily wanted coconut shampoo now.

"Okay, then." Kelley began, opening up a patient notes folder. It must have already had fifty pages bound into it. As Kelley flipped through, Emily could see hand-written notes with little drawings, printouts, typed notes and – she stopped at a glossy printed page with about a dozen 'ham-slice' images that she recognised as MRI scans.

"Again, thank you *so* much for volunteering for this study. I've transferred a hundred pounds to the account you wrote in your form this morning. Just a little thank-you for now."

"Oh, wow! That's– that's amazing, thank-you!" She could also feel Mads react.

Easy Money! She sent. It made Emily laugh involuntarily.

"So, to answer one of the *big* questions first. The DNA test from the mouth swab we did indicates that genetically, you're 100% Female, with normal X-X chromosomes.

"There's a condition, more common than previously thought catchily called forty-six, XY DSD: androgen insensitivity syndrome, or Morris Syndrome where about one in fifteen thousand women actually carry a male chromosome pattern, but during their early foetal growth their body didn't respond to the testosterone produced by their developing sex organs and they just go on to exhibit normal female growth.

It's quite fascinating... but that's not you."

Emily nodded, "So, I'm normal, but... not normal then?"

"Yeees, and no." Kelley made a weighing-up gesture with her hands. "The internal scans show largely normal female reproductive organs; that explains why you get your period as normal. But..."

Emily knew there would be a 'but' somewhere.

"Go on, I'm here for the full ride," she prompted.

Kelley nodded, a serious look on her face. "But, there is severe atrophy in your ovaries. The highest resolution scans show none of the normal egg follicle producing structures you'd expect. I'm so sorry, but that does mean that in all likelihood you're unlikely to be able to give birth naturally." She stopped to allow this to sink in, her kind eyes locked onto Emily's.

It wasn't really a surprise. "That's okay, I think I probably guessed that would be the case." She thought that actually hearing it, she might have had a stronger reaction but she felt genuinely at ease.

"But."

Another but? Emily tilted her head.

"But, it might not mean that you're precluded from actually becoming a *parent*," she said enigmatically.

"Huh?" It took a second or two for the implication to hit home, "You mean..." Now, *this* was unexpected.

"Please. Let's not jump the gun or anything, but at the moment I can't entirely rule it out."

"But I thought my *uniqueness* was just external, just an extra bit of flesh?"

"It would seem not." Kelley leaned her elbows on the desk and smiled. "You seem to have a very,

very rare condition. True hermaphroditism, where you have a complete, albeit not fully formed set of both female *and* male reproductive organs. It's more common for the external structures to appear, but as you very candidly and kindly disclosed on your questionnaire you say that you are capable of a 'male' discharge at orgasm."

Emily remembered that she'd ticked that box. "Yes, but I mean it's only a little – though," she shrugged, "I suppose, I don't really know what's normal."

"Oh, don't worry, there's no such thing as *normal*. People get too hung up about that," Kelley scoffed.

Emily nodded. Normal wasn't anything she had ever been used to.

"Now, I know that I said that there wouldn't be any physical examinations," Kelley began, carefully, "and that still holds. But the only way to be truly certain one way or another is if you were to be able to produce a sample for our fertility lab. We can arrange—"

"You want me to... um, you know?"

Kelley looked a little sheepish, but that just kind of made her look cute. The way her big red ponytail swung around and over her shoulder.

"I'll do it." Emily said firmly. "Like I said, I'm all in; we've come this far."

Kelley relaxed. "That's great – sorry." She turned to her computer and tapped, a tiny grin forming.

"I'll see if I can book you in for today, seeing as you're here." She finished with a dramatic click of her mouse and waited for the screen to update.

"Oh," she added sucking her teeth impatiently at the computer, "Do you find that you need to urinate more frequently than most people?"

"Er," Emily wasn't expecting that, "I guess so?" She thought a bit more about it, "Yes. I think I do. Why?"

Kelley flipped through the file of notes to one of the scan images, "You seem to have two bladders as well. They're sort of fused and the end result is a rather smaller capacity than just a single one."

Emily peered at the photograph, but it didn't make a lot of sense to her. "Huh. That figures."

"Ah, here we go." Kelley prodded at the screen, "They've only got a couple of bookings today, so you can just drop in any time you like. They'll be expecting you."

The Male fertility clinic was a modern looking building across the other side of the huge car park.

She appreciated the warmth inside after the chilly walk from the main building.

"Hi, I'm Emily Moon," she announced softly to the receptionist, "I was referred by—"

"Yes, Ms. Stranack. She called ahead to explain." The middle-aged woman at the desk smiled kindly, and produced a clear sample bottle which appeared to have already had a label printed on the side. "Take this and go through to the waiting area. We'll call you in next to save you having to wait."

Emily glanced apprehensively towards the seating area where two men were seated.

"Read this carefully first." The receptionist handed her a small, glossy booklet.

She took a seat in the corner of the room furthest

from the two men. They were both intensely engaged with their mobile phones, but each glanced up at Emily as she entered and found a place.

She busied herself with the little leaflet, mostly to avoid eye contact with the other patients. It talked mostly about hygiene; 'wash your hands and penis before and afterwards' and the mechanics of collecting the sample. She grimaced.

"What does it say?" Mads sent from her chain on Emily's rucksack – she'd forgotten she was there and jumped at the voice in her head.

"Don't." she replied silently, *"It's pretty grim."*

"Did you see those two guys looking at you when you came in? I wonder that they're thinking." Mads chuckled. *"I bet it's really messing with their heads seeing a woman in here."*

"Pack it in, Mads." Emily was getting a little anxious and Mads' jokes weren't helping. *"I bet they get trans people in here all the time, maybe even some like me. I mean, Kelley's running that study isn't she? I bet I'm not the first she's sent down here."*

"Hey, I hear they have loads of porn in the little room for... you know."

Emily didn't reply. The door at the end suddenly opened and a middle-aged man came out. Emily tried not to look at him, but her eyes followed him all the way out. He had a brown suede jacket on, balding, glasses. Why couldn't she stop watching him? She knew he must be kind of embarrassed, he looked at the floor all the way out, hands thrust into the pockets of his jacket.

"Moon." The Tannoy on the wall crackled.

Electricity jolted through her. She slowly got to her feet and silently walked to the door that the man had just come from.

She felt the eyes of the two men on her and realised with shame how she had stared at the guy when he left.

Emily stopped dead as she stepped through into what at first appeared to be a tiny cubicle. To the right was a counter with glass window – it reminded her a little of a bank counter.

A woman in a lab coat stepped up to the glass. Emily waved her plastic cup with a weak smile.

"Go through to the quiet room," the woman said. "You read the instructions?"

"Um, yeah."

"Okay." She nodded towards the other door in the chamber which had been unnoticed until now.

"... Okay." Hesitantly, she placed her hand on the door handle and ventured inside.

The room was a celebration of beige. The whole place just seemed... seedy. Mismatched furniture sat against the walls, upon one of which hung an elaborately framed print that made her snort with laughter. Surely, hung there with a wicked sense of irony. A classical painting of some woman by a pool, naked, combing her hair while cherubs looked on adoringly.

She shook her head and looked around. A couch, a coffee table with a neat pile of magazines, box of tissues, wipes. Opposite, a small sink with hospital type pedal bin.

There was a single bed. Emily unclipped Mads, set

her down and sat on the edge of the bed to take off her boots.

"I guess this will do. Shit, this place smells... musty." She unhitched her skirt and slipped off her underwear, sighing as she placed them neatly on the coffee table.

Eyeing the bed warily, she washed, and picked up what she hoped was a clean towel from by the sink and laid it neatly on the bed before making herself comfortable.

At least it was nice and warm in here. It made it a little easier as she got underway.

"Hey! Check this out!" Mads shouted. Emily had to look up to see where she was; the voice in her head had no direction to it.

Mads was dragging one of the magazines from the table over towards the bed, "Look! This is absolutely filthy!"

"Shit, Mads, you're not helping. Put it back." Her hands stopped moving and she let her head fall back onto the lumpy pillow.

"If you'd have known, you could have brought Bruce. That always does the trick. You know you love good old Bruce Willies, don't you?" She dropped the magazine and hopped up onto the bed and admired the results of her saucy taunting, "There you go. You're getting there."

Several minutes later, Emily passed the tissue-wrapped container under the gap in the glass. She'd managed to awkwardly catch her half teaspoon. Mads fussed about with tissues and wipes afterwards – she had to admit to enjoying feeling a little pampered.

Still slightly flushed, she made her own walk of shame past the two guys in the waiting room. She smiled a little at the perplexed look on one of their faces. *Ha, you'll just have to keep guessing buster,* she thought to herself.

CHAPTER 10

THIS TIME, EMILY tried napping in the afternoon then waking again around 1am. She hoped this would give her a little more time to come to her senses.

Mads hopped about happily on the table while Emily ate some... breakfast?

"It's going to be good to finally get some payback on those gits," Mads said. "I know it won't change what happened, or undo the hurt they did to us both, but at least it's *something*."

"You know," Emily put down the half-eaten mince pie, "I'd pretty much gotten over it. If it wasn't for seeing them in the pub at Christmas, I'd have been okay."

"You're more forgiving than me then."

"But it all came back pretty quickly, remember? I got a flashback when Ian came over to us."

"Oh, shit yeah," Mads said excitedly, "That all makes sense. I thought he was having a stroke or something – that was you?"

"Yeah, didn't know it at the time though." She paused in thought. "I should get you charged up before you go out then," she said with a little sigh. "Come on."

Mads hopped off the table and Emily caught her in her arms. She cradled her against her bosom and began to let the power flow into her. It came so naturally again along with the overwhelming feeling of warmth and love. But at least after the diagnosis from Kelley, she had the answers to her speculations about ever being a mother. A strange feeling washed through her; well at least a *mother*, her other results weren't due until the new year.

What if... what if we could use this magic to bring back Mads' body? Could we start a family?

She felt a pang of disappointment when the flow of power slowed and stopped.

"You okay?" Mads asked quietly.

"Yeah." She lifted Mads up and placed her carefully back on the table in front of her.

"Are you sure?"

"Really. Yes, don't worry. Just a little tired." She pushed the remainder of the mince pie into her mouth and washed it down with a gulp of hot chocolate.

"Gabriel?" Mads asked, "If Em has to feed me every day like this isn't it going to make her sick?"

The stone creature stirred in his armchair, "Every

day? Maybe. But the climbing and running take their toll. You don't need to feed every day if you lead a sedentary life."

Emily looked relieved.

"But," he continued, "You can keep a store of energy. A vast amount if you wanted to. Take a little every day, stock it up." He sat up now, "Take from others if you will it."

"Whoah, hang on. Am I some kind of vampire voodoo doll now?" Mads exclaimed in horror.

Gabriel snorted loudly, "My dear, there are no such things as vampires, believe me."

"Well, what do you mean by *take* it from others?" This sounded a little sinister to Mads, but if it meant not having to drain the very life out of Emily, then she wanted to know more.

"You are also by half, a creature of magic. A human soul bound to a token, but the power runs through you as the roots of a tree hold it to the ground." He crawled closer, and up onto the arm of the couch to Emily's left. "You are imbued with a little control over the power that flows through you. If you will it, you can take it, hold it, give it."

"Aha, so a voodoo powerbank then!" Emily chuckled.

Mads turned and, although her stitched face wasn't especially expressive just yet, there was a definite scowl.

"Sorry, sorry, sorry." Emily begged, though holding back her giggles.

"So, does it just work the same way as Em does *her* magic? I just have to think it?"

"Precisely that," the gargoyle said, with more than a little satisfaction in his voice.

"Then I want to go back again and pay Ian a visit first." Mads said with the kind of determination that was very hard to argue with.

"Okay, okay," Emily conceded, "So long as we go mess up Scott's head right after."

The time had come to send Mads out on her mission of retribution again.

Emily had her scarf ready and packed her sides with pillows to stop her from toppling over. Gabriel took up station on the coffee table, cross-legged. It wasn't a pretty sight, whoever had carved him all those hundreds of years ago seemed to be compensating for something, Emily thought to herself.

"Remember, prop the letterbox open and push a box against the door," Emily fussed.

Mads had an old sock tied around her waist which she would ball-up and stuff into the letterbox.

"Okay, let's do this," Emily said through gritted teeth.

Gabriel ambled off the table and over to the door to let Mads out. She waited patiently outside while Gabriel returned to the coffee table.

"Mistress, if you would be so kind."

"Just a moment." Emily fixed the gargoyle in her gaze. She wasn't using farsight just yet, so it was just the two of them. "What would it take to conjure up a new body for Mads using this... magic?"

The stone creature scratched at his mossy chin and made all the appearance of sighing.

"My lady, that would take such power as even I have never seen. You would need to gather a vast reserve – I wager that your poppet can surely accommodate, but to *wield* that power?" He leaned a little closer; a curious grin had started to creep across his face. "It would destroy you."

Emily was crestfallen, "So there's no hope?" she said sadly.

"Oh. I didn't say that it could not be done. Just not by *you*. There is only one other that I know–" he hesitated, "– knew. But that would be my past mistress, and she is of course... Indisposed."

"Why would she help us? Even if she was still alive." Emily sat back on the couch, "She fried that night with Mads and me didn't she?"

"True, she was *fried*, as you say it. But her goose was not entirely cooked," he said with a cackle in his voice.

"What happened? Tell me, how can we get her to help us?" she pleaded.

The gargoyle sat up straight and wrapped his tail around himself. "This is for later. We have business tonight."

Emily suddenly remembered that Mads had been waiting outside in the cold.

"Okay, but look, we need to talk about this afterwards."

Gabriel tugged at an imaginary forelock, "As you wish."

"Mads, sorry... I had to pee," she sent.

Emily lowered her blindfold and patched Gabriel in on the farsight feed.

"Okay, off you go." And in an instant she was bounding down the stairwell.

Her flight across the car park seemed quicker than last time. Was it because she was fully charged, or because the route was familiar?

The stairwell was unoccupied this time, so Mads darted inside and scampered up the steps.

Emily kept count of the levels while Mads took care of navigating the trash and dark spots where the lights had failed.

"This one," Mads sent, and they flew out of the stairwell and out onto the walkway in front of the flats.

They reached Ian's door in a moment. There were no lights from any of the windows.

Mads untied the sock from herself, rolled it up into a ball and leapt. She hung onto the knocker underneath the flap of the letterbox and pushed the sock ball inside, wedging it open.

She wriggled through being careful not to dislodge the sock and dropped silently to the floor below.

The boxes were still there, so her priority was to secure her means of escape and push one under the door.

Just as she was about to creep to Ian's room to the left at the end of the corridor she stopped dead.

"You've got to be kidding me!" Emily called out.

"I know these things." Gabriel said calmly. "But I have never seen the need in such numbers."

All down the dark corridor, Ian had placed mouse traps. It seemed that he had been expecting them – or someone. But whoever he had been anticipating to return would have been human sized because Mads was able to pick her way easily between the traps.

"Where the hell did he get thirty-odd mouse-traps this time of year?" Emily sent.

"Dunno," Mads replied, clearly amused. *"Maybe that's what's in all these boxes, or more knives. Looks like he's turned out to be a bit of a Del-Boy – hang, on I've got an idea."*

Carefully, Mads pushed about six of the traps along the filthy carpet and left them scattered outside Ian's bedroom door.

The door was closed, but not on the latch so Mads only had to slowly push it open. It dragged against the carpet, but thankfully didn't creak.

Looking about the room, Mads saw that it was an absolute tip; clothes, boxes, trash lay strewn about the room. A gentle snore issued from the double bed, which Mads climbed easily.

Ian lay alone in the middle of the bed.

Silently, Mads crept along the side until she was level with his chest. He lay face up, mouth half open deep in sleep.

Emily held her breath as Mads slowly crawled up onto his chest on all fours. Mads of course didn't breathe, so made no sound at all.

She reached the middle of his chest without discovery, then climbed just a little higher so she could see his face. The only sound in the room was Ian's breathing; the faintest of light seeped through the thick, grimy curtains leaving the room in almost complete pitch blackness.

But Mads' eyes could see his piggy face in perfect

detail. Emily shuddered and let out her breath slowly.

"You ready?" She sent.

"Now or never," came the silent reply.

Remembering the warm, nourishing feeling that flowed over her when Emily had fed her, she cast a picture of the same happening right now in her mind.

Almost instantly, a faint golden thread began to drift from Ian's open mouth. It snaked through the air like cigarette smoke and wound itself around her body.

Another joined it, then another until half a dozen gently swaying tendrils of energy twisted and turned in the air between them.

The feeling was like no other. Like warm chocolate melting in her mouth, except that the feeling spread through her entire tiny body.

For two, maybe three minutes, Mads fed on the pure life energy of the disgusting man. She could feel it filling her up, but as Gabriel had suggested, her appetite felt almost infinite.

"I think you should stop now." Emily sent. But her words were lost in the ecstasy of feeding. Another two tendrils had joined the link, and they all pulsed with exquisite life.

"Mads! You should stop." Came Emily's voice in her head. But she didn't want to stop.

Then, with her mind Emily reached out and yanked the tendrils away. The connection broke suddenly in a brilliant flash of golden light.

In that instant Mads came to and Ian's eyes snapped open to briefly see her face looming over his. Eyes black as coal.

She leapt off his chest and was at the door before

the first yell could pass his lips. But it was a hoarse and strangled sound as he lay briefly paralysed by the narcotic effect of her feeding.

His body began to shake and convulse as his nerves scrambled to reconnect, to save him from this horror.

Burned into his retinas from the bright flash, slowly turning negative was the face of the girl who had died a few days ago near the pub. The girl that he had tormented for years, the one who his very last words to had been full of hatred and spite.

She was dead. But here she was, still floating as an after-image in his eyeballs. Blinking, shutting his eyes tightly wouldn't make the face go away.

As the sense slowly returned to his body, Ian lay exhausted and sobbing in his bed.

Mads had by now bounded from the apartment, trailing the sock and was hiding in the shadows near the stairwell.

Had she waited to watch or gloat, the exquisite justice that he had wet himself in fear would not have been lost on either girl.

"Holy shit!" Emily yelled, gasping for breath and laughing with the thrill of the narrow escape, "His FACE!"

"Like he saw a ghost, yeah?" Mads whooped silently. *"We got him good and proper – the little fucker!"*

"But Mads," Emily said under her breath and through the aether, "You almost killed him. You went too far."

Mads sobered a little, *"I can't say I'm sorry Em,"* She sent, *"I don't care if I drain him dry, but Em, it*

143

just felt so good."

"I get it. I know how the flow feels. But we have to be careful. We're only out to mess with them, remember?"

"What does it matter if one arse-prod less walks the Earth?" Gabriel cut in.

"No!" Emily snapped, icily, "We're not killers. Understand?"

"He's got a point, Em."

"No. Just because they don't have a sense of decency, we don't let them drag us down with them."

Two floors down, it was much the same with Scott. The layout of the flat was identical – they all were in this block. His abode was far cleaner, though there were still signs of drug-taking in the bedroom.

The feeding was more restrained this time, though Mads felt a snap of resentment when Emily prompted her to stop. She climbed down from his curled up form and wandered out into the hallway. There was no urgency, Scott was sleeping peacefully.

The door to the living room was closed, but it was no trouble to leap up to the door handle and with her back against the door frame, push it down with her feet. The door opened smoothly into the room, lit by the slowly changing lights of a half-heartedly decorated plastic Christmas tree.

"Dumb-ass! Doesn't he know it's dangerous to leave decorations on unattended?" Mads silently grumbled. *"I wouldn't give a monkey's if this little shit burned in his house, but he's putting others at risk too."* With that, she pulled the plug out and plunged

144

the room into darkness.

A human eye might have taken a few minutes to adjust, but Mads' supernatural sight instantly saw the room in a light that seemed to go beyond mere colours and shade.

What Mads saw when she looked around the room made Emily gasp.

It wasn't the drugs paraphernalia abandoned on the table in front of the unreasonably large TV, though Mads did feel a tug of envy at the massive screen; the drugs were to be expected from a waster like Scott.

No, it was the little bags of pills and neat stacks of cash arrayed on a large dining table that had shocked them so.

"Fuck." Emily breathed, "Scott's a bloody *dealer*."

"Absolute tosser," sent Mads as she wandered around the table. Cash was piled up like bales of hay around her. She paused, then seemed to have made her mind up about something. *"I'm gonna teach this wanker a lesson,"* she sent then began stuffing the sock she had been trailing about with money.

"You do realise what this is going to mean, don't you?" Emily said. "This isn't all *his* money, it's going to belong to whoever he's getting his crap from."

"Too right," Mads sent. Emily could feel the anger across the aether, *"They're going to come round and break his legs. And I want him to know that it was me that set him up."* She began kicking the bags of pills onto the floor then pushed the rest of the money into a crude 'M' shape on the table.

"You could just take his whole life force." Gabriel had been silent throughout, but chimed in.

"No, Em's right. We're not killers, though I really should just end this little fuck-weasel right now. I'll come back tomorrow and the day after and the day after that. Run him down so low, and watch him wonder when the knock on the door is going to come."

Gabriel cackled and rubbed his clawed hands together with glee, "What exquisite torture!"

"Get your arse out of bed!" Scott yelled through Ian's letterbox then continued pounding on the door. He stood back and sucked his teeth, looking nervously up and down the walkway. The curtains twitched at the bedroom window. He jumped to it and slammed it with the palm of his hand.

"Hurry up!" then muttered "fucker," under his breath. Sounds of movement from inside, followed by a muffled yelling and banging around.

"The fuck's he doing in there?" he said to himself, then pounded on the door again until it opened.

A pale and dishevelled figure appeared at a crack in the door, "What?" he said plaintively.

"Can't you answer your phone, bruh?" Scott whined, moving anxiously from foot to foot like he needed to piss.

"Battery? Why what's up?"

"Put ya shoes on and come with me," he growled, "Your fucking ghost's paid me a visit, innit."

The door closed, then opened again several seconds later. Scott had thrown on a black gilette, though his arms were bare with the dirty t-shirt underneath. He shivered and blew a cloud of icy breath into the morning air.

Scott set off without a word, but looked back when he noticed Ian was lagging.

"What you done? You're limping," he grumbled.

Ian didn't reply, but shot a poisonous scowl after Scott as he vanished into the gloomy stairwell.

"Look!" Scott pointed at the cash on his table, "Look at this shit."

Ian approached the table warily as if it might have been covered with venomous snakes. He let out a shuddering breath.

"And your door was locked and all?"

"Course it was fuckin' locked, you spaz!" Scott turned and yelled. He wiped a fleck of spittle from his chin then drew a long breath in from his nose. "How come it's all in this 'M' shape?"

Ian shook his head slowly, "I told ya. Fuckin' ghost." He bent down to look across the mounds of banknotes. "Did you see her," he said without looking up.

"Nah. You were trippin' there's no ghosts. But some fucker was in here last night and I think there's money missing."

"Did you count it?" Ian stood up and pushed a packet of pills on the floor with his foot as if it might be alive.

"No, I..."

"Mate, you was scared innit!"

"Kiss it, bro. I know how much oughta be there. It's definitely light."

"You think it could have been her girl did it?" Ian asked.

"Nah, she's in hospital. Didn't you see? She was pretty fucked-up that night. Crispy!" He smirked evilly.

Ian looked at the table and let out a long sigh, "Then we're fucked." He ran his fingers through his greasy hair.

"Billy Whizz is gonna want his money tomorrow," Scott whined.

"Can't we just give him what we got and say we ain't sold all the pills yet?"

"Don't be a muppet, we said we'd sell the lot. If we don't prove we can do it, he'll drop us like a turd."

The two stood in silence for a minute contemplating the consequences of letting down a maniac like Billy on their very first deal.

"Okay." Scott had reached a decision, "We hold a party, flog everything we can and take a loss. What's missing is just gonna come out of our cut."

Ian winced and started scooping up the little bags of purple pills from the floor. "There must be about fifty hits here still, you sure we can shift 'em all?"

"Hope so." Scott had started to gather up all the cash and was counting it, placing it in neat bundles on the table. "We just call in all, and I mean *all* the punters we used to sell J's shit to. Call it a new year's party."

"Guess so, we done it before. Get some banging tunes, should be sweet..." He crouched to get the last packet from under the table, "Fifty-three," he declared.

Scott had finished counting, "So, how much we short?" Ian Asked.

"Three hundred and twenty pounds!" Emily cried, slapping the last note onto the table with the rest recovered from Mads' sock-haul.

"I think we're set for a while, what with the money you're getting from your cute doctor friend."

Emily gave her a look, but Mads just chuckled and threw herself into the pile of money and rolled about in it. She stopped and sat up, "Always wanted to do that, much easier when you're my size."

The last of the fireworks lit up the London skyline in a breath-taking blaze of colour. Emily raised her cider can for Mads to fist-bump from where she sat perched on her shoulder.

"Happy New Year, Em," she said, "It's going to be a weird one, that's for sure."

"Remember when you said you were sure it was going to be a good year when it turned twenty nineteen?"

Mads grunted, "Yeah. Got that wrong, didn't I?"

"Yep," Emily chuckled and took a swig from her can, "Think you've nailed the prediction for twenty twenty-three though."

Emily flipped channels on the TV. Jules Holland was just starting to get into full swing with a band she'd never heard of, but she liked the sound.

"You think we can really conjure up a new body for me?" Mads asked suddenly.

Emily let out a long breath and turned her head to face Mads' little black eyes. "Hope so. I guess Gabriel knows what he's talking about. We just have to save up enough energy." She called across the room, "Isn't that right?"

The armchair creaked slightly in the dark corner and a pair of pointy ears emerged from the shadow, "Indeed mistress. Will you send your poppet out again tonight to collect?"

There was a pause while Emily weighed it up. "I don't know, I'm pretty tired and I'd think that those two gits would be out at some rave or other pushing their drugs."

"I don't mind going," Mads said.

"Yeah, but you're getting to be a bit of a power junkie yourself."

"Rest then." Gabriel said smoothly. "Let me go stand watch, then when their revels are done I'll return to rouse you both."

Mads climbed down into Emily's lap and looked up at her, "That does make sense, doesn't it?"

Nobody noticed the inert form clinging like a limpet against the concrete pillar outside Scott's apartment. Though, quite honestly if anyone had seen him, they would have happily dismissed him as some psychedelic artefact of the absurd quantities of drugs and alcohol that were being consumed inside and along the walkway.

Most of the flats on this section were empty, some boarded up with perforated steel plates and adorned with graffiti. So no bother from immediate neighbours.

A low throb of music bled out into the cold air, brightening to an unholy cacophony of noise and light and smoke whenever someone came or went.

Inside, Scott was the lord of misrule; host,

magician, everybody's bosom buddy. He strutted and schmoozed, dispensing little purple pellets of distraction to all that waved their money his way.

Ian had a cunning enterprise of his own which Scott had uncharacteristically complemented him on. By the end of the night, he would have more than made up for their shortfall giving away free shots of cheap, likely counterfeit, even more likely toxic vodka to their 'guests', then stinging them for the abusively overpriced cans of energy drink they craved when the drugs crashed their blood-sugar level.

This was perhaps to be Ian's finest hour.

The last of Scott's houseguests were quietly shown the door at a little after five in the morning.

There had been a light flurry of snow about an hour earlier and that had persuaded the handful of revellers out on the walkway to go home or seek somewhere warmer or find anywhere that a can of warm drink didn't cost them a tenner.

Gabriel hadn't shifted a millimetre all night. He continued watching the apartment from above for another half an hour until Ian finally emerged. He took a deep breath of the cold air and let it out in a self-satisfied cloud of vapour. They had done it; they had sold the entire stock of pills and made a tidy profit.

He felt for the tight roll of notes in his pocket and started on his way home.

The block was silent again, and in that silence, a shadow slowly moved. A dusting of snow dropped from it as it unfolded and took up a position closer to

Scott's bedroom window.

The curtains were open. Scott took one last draw from a joint before kicking his shoes into the corner of the room and turning off the light. He threw himself onto the bed and was asleep in seconds.

The stone lookout scuttled down the side of the building quick as a lizard and bounded back to the girls' flat.

The key was hidden in a secret place that only a gargoyle could have reached, and with it he let himself in.

The bedroom was dark to human sight. Gabriel lingered a moment to watch the two sleeping figures on the bed. Sleeping, he noted. Often such soul-bound tokens could only ape human response. Most never truly slept. This one was very well made and he allowed himself what passed for satisfaction in his synthetic being.

He climbed to the head of the bed and crouched on an unoccupied pillow.

"Mistress. Awaken now."

Mads sprang up from the pillow where she slept next to Emily's Head.

"Shit. Sorry, it's only you." She seemed genuinely startled.

Emily stirred.

"Em. It's time. Gabriel's back." She climbed over to the bedside table to find Emily's phone, but her mitten-hands were too clumsy for the tiny buttons on the side.

Emily reached sleepily over to grasp the phone and squinted at the time on the screen. She yawned vastly and scratched at her head as she heaved herself up into a sitting position. Her hair was all over the place.

"Okay then. Late-shift," she mumbled and drifted to the kitchen to find coffee. Mads hopped eagerly afterwards followed by Gabriel, who padded behind like a loyal (but damned ugly) dog.

Mads again stole into Scott's bedroom after picking her way through the litter left behind by the party before.

"Must have been quite a bash," Mads sent as the bedroom door opened.

She climbed straight up and found him sleeping on his back. Silently, she mounted his chest and leaned over as before to get closer to his face.

The transfer began and once more, exquisite energy twisted through the air in golden throbbing ropes. Emily felt it too and sighed gently as the feeling washed over her.

Without warning, the flow stuttered and Scott's chest heaved, throwing Mads off onto the bed.

"What happened? I didn't break the connection," Mads sent. In the darkness, Scott convulsed again and a thin line of foam ran from the corner of his mouth.

"Is he having a seizure?" Emily cried. "Oh, God, what do we do?"

Mads watched him for a few seconds before replying. *"No, I think he's overdosed on something."* There was a wrapper on the bed which she recognised from the first night. *"He's been taking his own junk, the idiot!"*

"He's choking, Mads!"

"I can see that," she replied coldly.

"Aren't you going to help him?" Emily was starting to get frantic now. Scott had stopped shaking.

"He–" Emily caught her breath, "He's not breathing."

Slowly, a delicate wisp of gold began to rise from Scott's open mouth.

"Command your poppet to catch this," Gabriel said with grave urgency. "There is nothing more to be done, but to waste this would be a great loss."

"Why? What's happening?" Emily said in confusion.

"I heard him," Mads sent, *"I get it."* She climbed back up onto the chest of the dying man and simply invited the thread to join her. It did so, connecting and flowing into her.

Suddenly, the delicate tendril of energy burst into five, six writhing branches of blinding golden light each one as thick as a human arm.

The effect was incomprehensible, an entire human life-force was being dumped in one blast into Mads' tiny body. The ecstasy of bleeding off a small quantity of energy was pure and complete pleasure, but magnify that by a hundred, two hundred, more even?

The feedback caused Emily to cry out and gasp. Gabriel watched on, hopping heavily on his chair in glee like a monkey.

When it was over, Emily realised that she had broken connection with Mads. Her head fizzed as if it were full of popping candy, somewhere in the distance a neighbour thumped on the wall.

"Oh my God," Emily whispered, "What have we done?"

There was no reply, everything was black under the

scarf. A cold surge of panic swept over her.

She had lost contact with Mads.

Still breathless, she tore off the blindfold and rubbed her eyes, "Gabriel, what just happened?"

A voice right against her ear made her jump, "The boy died." The gargoyle said simply. "What had to be done was done. It was his own doing, you are blameless in all of this. But we now have his life force." He chuckled softly, "A most marvellous prize, don't you think?"

Emily was filled with disgust, "He died? Oh God, he was a shit but I never wanted this."

"You are without blame," Gabriel reiterated, "He died at his own hand with his own foul poisons."

"I need to contact Mads," she said pulling the scarf back over her eyes. Nothing came, she growled with frustration.

"Be calm, mistress and reach out gently."

Emily took a deep breath and let it out slowly, feeling for Mads with her mind.

Slowly, a fizz of dim colours resolved into an image. She was in near-darkness again.

"Mads, oh thank God. I'm back, are you okay?" she sent.

"Amazing!" Came the reply, *"We need more. I'm going after Ian, I'm in his hallway."*

"No, Mads, stop. We can't do this. It's not right!"

"Bullshit, Em! They were both lowlife, they deserve this."

"No. Nobody has to die. We're not like them."

"We need the energy, Em."

"We can get it another way, it'll just take a little

longer."

"But they DESERVE this. They deserve to die."

"Yes, he deserves to be punished, of course he does, but we can do better than just killing him. We can be *smart* about this. Let me think."

Emily could feel Mads sigh to herself. She crawled behind a box in the hallway and glared down the corridor. The TV seemed to be on in the living room. Perhaps she was being a little rash.

"Okay, okay... I think that energy stuff kind of went to my head. Ian's still awake anyhow."

"You could have been caught!" Emily cried.

She was right, of course.

"Okay, okay. Look Scott's dead, he overdosed or something." Emily reasoned, "What if we get Ian implicated in that? We can get him locked up, even if it's just for the drugs and stuff."

Mads thought about this, Emily was right again – of course. *"Okay, so what's the plan?"*

"Can you get his wallet without being spotted?" Emily asked, still thinking on her feet.

"Um, yeah, I think that's his jacket on the floor here. Messy git." She stepped out from behind the box and rummaged in the gilette.

Luck was with her. Zipped up in a pocket was a tatty wallet. Emily saw this.

"Okay, find a credit card and bring it down to Scott's."

She did as instructed, leaving her balled-up sock in the letterbox so she could return silently. Along the way, Emily explained the plan.

"You ARE a smart little chicken," she chuckled

when she had finished.

"Are you sure you're happy about this bit?" Emily asked, as Mads dragged a large knife across the floor from the Kitchen to Scott's room.

"I think I'd regard this as THERAPY," she sent gleefully.

It wasn't that the knife was too heavy for Mads to carry, it was just a matter of weight ratio – the carving knife probably weighed as much as she did, so dragging it was pretty much the only way to move it.

She hopped clumsily up onto the bed where Scott's body lay and up onto his chest. The knife was unwieldy, so she leapt into the air with the knife and landed with it point-down square in the middle of Scott's chest. It glanced off a rib, bounced and clattered to the floor.

This was going to be harder than she had imagined.

Perhaps somewhere softer? Remembering her hammer-throw skills from school, she swung the knife round and round making satisfying slashes to his face and neck.

Of course, there was only a moderate amount of blood what with him being already dead, but this would be sufficient for Emily's plan.

Using a piece of kitchen towel, she soaked it in the blood which was now oozing quite satisfactorily from the wounds.

Just for effect, she then stabbed the knife into his chest until it eventually remained standing proudly.

Next, she ran back to the hallway and retrieved the credit card she had taken from Ian's wallet and found

Scott's phone.

Using his still warm finger to unlock it, she ordered two large meat-tastic pizzas from the all-night place round the corner.

"How the hell did you know he'd have the app on his phone, Em?" She sent. The phone's screen wouldn't react to her cloth hands, so it was a slow process to dab dead fingers on the phone. At least she wouldn't be leaving any fingerprints behind.

"You didn't see the big pile of boxes chucked outside his door? Anyone that lazy won't be arsed to go walk for a pizza."

Mads shook her head, marvelling. *"Amazing."*

Even more amazing that a pizza place would still be open at nearly six in the morning on New Year's Day.

With that done, she stepped back to make sure the knife was still in place – it had sagged a little, but it would have to do as a statement.

The last part of the plan was easy; race back up the steps, dab a little of the blood on Ian's door from the towel and pop the damning evidence and credit card through the letterbox.

She tied the sock round her head, ninja-style and leapt from the eighth story balcony.

Emily hated her for that.

Twenty minutes later, a young, tired pizza delivery boy stood gawping outside Scott's blood-stained door. He pulled his phone from his jacket pocket and began dialling.

CHAPTER 11

WHEN MADS RETURNED, the first thing that Emily did was to clean her again.

It was very cold out, so she hadn't picked up a lot of dirt from the frozen ground. Her heart-stopping dive from Ian's walkway had landed her in a shallow drift of pristine, powdery snow. She had just shaken that off and scampered back to the flat.

Emily had opened the door to her when she arrived to find little bobbles of snow clinging to her feet and ankles (such as they were).

Enjoying a little of their newfound wealth, Emily braved the expense and pulled out the little bar-radiator. They sat on the couch in the lovely orange glow as Mads dried off.

It was truly cosy, almost like... *before*.

In lieu of a more conventionally intimate moment, Emily had fed Mads for a minute or two and once more they had felt the delicious togetherness it brought them.

The foil from the last of the mince pies lay crumpled on the coffee table and Emily sipped at her hot chocolate. Mads basked on Emily's chest and they talked about what might unfold in their future.

"You're right," Emily conceded with a sigh, "If we *do* bring you back you'd have to spend the whole of your life in hiding."

Mads examined her hand, "Not that I could walk about like this though."

"But at least you won't have to see a doctor or use any kind of ID or passport. If we go on holiday, I can just pop you in my bag."

Mads chuckled, "We'd save a fortune." She paused reflectively, "But I miss your touch, your smell. I'd never be able to hold you like I used to."

"Oh, I don't know any more." Emily made a little, frustrated growl. "Maybe we should just try it. I mean, the authorities would just have to... just figure it out."

"And if we can't get my body back, then at least we have this." She turned over and looked into Emily's eyes, her tiny black beads seemed to have an expression of hope."

"We also need to get a handle on this power-lust. I almost lost you when Scott died, and I could never go through that again. It was taking you over."

"So quickly too," Mads agreed. "I wonder if that gargoyle is a bad influence."

He shifted in his armchair as if to remind them that he was still there and he could hear them.

Emily looked over to the corner of the room where he lurked in the shadows.

"Gabriel, come over here, would you please."

Silently, he obliged and climbed up onto the coffee table where he sat cross-legged, tail in his lap. He tilted his head and replied sweetly, "Mistress?"

"We need to get some clear answers." Emily said, taking charge at last. She felt a buzz of anticipation.

"I think we really need to take control of the situation now. Scott's gone, I didn't want that, and now I hope Ian's going to be put away for a very long time. I think we're good on that account now."

Gabriel hadn't shifted; his head remained tilted, listening patiently to what Emily had to say.

"So, you say that we can somehow get a new body for Mads. But it's going to need a *lot* more power, right?"

He nodded.

"There's to be no more killing, do you understand?"

"But Mistress, the amount of power you would need to grow an entire living body—"

"We can wait." Emily said firmly.

"It would be like filling a lake with a teaspoon." He protested, ears folded back like a scolded dog.

"I don't trust him," Mads cut in.

Gabriel turned in a flash and snarled. "You have no business in this."

"Don't you DARE!" Emily snapped back. "You don't talk to Mads like that. Do you understand?"

Gabriel flattened himself against the table in

castigation.

She leaned towards her familiar and spoke, low and deliberately, "Now. Tell me, truthfully why you are pushing us to gather so much power so quickly."

The gargoyle seemed to shrink a little and pulled himself into a tight knot on the table. He mumbled and squirmed.

"Tell me. You know you have to do whatever I tell you."

His head slowly rose up, he seemed to have made his eyes a little larger, a little more pathetic looking but Emily wasn't fooled.

"Forgive me Mistress, pretty mistress. I have deceived you—"

"Did you lie about bringing Mads back?" Emily cut across him calmly.

"Never! No, I didn't lie. You can bring your best beloved back, but..."

"Out with it."

He sighed and wrung his hands, "But the path is not an easy one. There is an onerous and perilous task to perform before we can even think to begin."

"I said no more killing," she warned.

"There is no other way, my Mistress."

"I won't do it. I won't be a part of any more evil doings. I should just dismiss you and send you on your way. We can manage by ourselves."

The stone imp made a pitiful keening sound and got onto its knees, pleading, "Please, no not that. It would mean the end of me."

"Why?" she asked simply.

He looked back in terror; he had to tell her the truth.

"Kind Mistress," he began meekly, "If I am not in service then I will quickly perish."

Again, "Why?"

"My reserves of life power will wain and I will return to inert stone." He finished with a dramatic shudder.

"I just realised. I've never seen you feed or anything. Where do you get your power from then?"

A pause. He looked back at Emily fearfully, then squeaked, "From *you* Mistress."

"Ha! I knew it!" Mads leapt onto the back of the couch and pointed an accusatory mitt at the cowering figure on the table. "I knew he was up to no good. You little fucker, you've been bleeding Em all this time, haven't you?"

He looked back reproachfully, but he knew not to answer back. His life was on the line here.

"Oh, pretty mistress," he fawned, "Oh giver of life, oh sweet desire to turn the hearts of all men..." he backpaddled, "and even lusty womenfolk."

"Shitbag," Mads growled.

"All that I take from you is just crumbs from the table. Enough only to move my limbs, to think my thoughts and to serve you." He prepared himself to say what needed to be said. "You must do one terrible thing if you want to hold your beloved like you ache to do. You must confront and kill Juliana, the witch, my former mistress, she who has brought this curse upon you."

"Kill her?" Emily gasped. "You didn't say anything about killing her, you said she would help us."

"Alas, no. She would never do that. Remember the

alley? She was out to kill *you*."

"But why? Why pick on us?"

"Just you. She could sense that you felt her power, she told me that you would give her away, expose her to others.

"No, the only way is to find where she is hiding. She's weak, but she will heal in time so you cannot wait. Once you have struck the deathblow, you can take her energy, conjure the flesh you crave."

"But how would I fight her? I can't just sneak up on her sickbed and stab her. Mads can't do that either. Besides, we don't know where she is... or have you known all along?"

Gabriel relaxed a little, he seemed to be off the hook for now. "I don't know where she is, but we might be able to track her down. I was her only familiar, so she has nothing to send out to gather energy for her. But she has a way, one she has been using for years."

"Her drugs." Mads said suddenly. "She's taking people's energy through the drugs she sells, am I right?"

The lecherous stone face grinned, "Exactly right, poppet. Each desperate fool that breathes in the vapours from her potions passes a little of themselves back to the witch herself."

"So, you think she's still selling her drugs? To heal herself?" Mads said, "It doesn't look like it. The old pushers must have moved back in by the looks of what Scott and Ian got themselves into."

"If she is then we could follow the pushers to where she's hiding out," Emily offered.

Gabriel sat up now, his ears had pricked up and he

was looking a lot more cheerful. "Clever Mistress." He began, then looked to Mads, ears dipping a little, "And her heart's gleam."

She scowled back, or at least it seemed she did.

"We could do a stakeout at the Greyhound. That's where she used to hang out," Mads suggested. "There's bound to be plenty of junkies sniffing about there looking for a fix."

"I'm not sure I want to go back into that dive again," Emily said.

"Okay. You know that carpet place next door. Well, used to be a carpet place – closed now. It's got a flat roof, we can sit up there in the dark, see everything." She paused for a beat, "Even all along that alley where..." she trailed off.

Emily grabbed her from the back of the couch and held her tightly. "Okay then. Let's do it."

An iron ladder lead from the fated alleyway up to the roof of the old store. It was rusty and it creaked at every step, but it carried Emily's slight frame without mishap.

From the corner at front of the building, they could clearly see the car park of the grubby pub, the entrance and much of the alley.

Emily had the forethought to drag a flattened cardboard box up from the trash outside the pub and lay it out on the grimy roof to kneel on.

Gabriel had scaled the wall by himself and was crouched low on the parapet glaring down at the empty street below.

"How long do you think we've got to sit here?"

Emily asked, already feeling the cold through her black puffer jacket.

"Dunno," Mads replied. She was laying on the low wall next to Gabriel, looking over the edge. "Used to see junkies come and go at all times, not long probably."

As if on cue, a clattering heap of a car pulled up in front of the pub and disgorged a scruffy looking young man. He hefted a backpack over his shoulder from the back seat and sauntered over to the concrete rings as the car spluttered away.

The three watched closely as he sat on the edge and lit a cigarette, blowing a huge cloud of smoke and frosty breath into the air above him.

"This looks like our guy," Mads sent in silence.

"Wait, let's just be sure." Emily urged in a low whisper.

Not more than a minute later, two men emerged from the pub and made a beeline for the potential pusher.

They didn't seem to care about finding a dark corner to do their deal; this kind of thing was so commonplace around here Emily lamented to herself.

Before long, the pusher opened up his bag and produced a sample of his wares. At this, the two began shouting loudly at the vendor. One produced what looked like a knife – were they going to rob him?

Emily ducked down low; this was getting dangerous.

"Shit!" Mads sent, *"They're kicking his arse out there. Look!"*

Emily peeped up over the parapet to see the pusher

backing away, almost tripping, from the two from the pub. They hurled the bag at him which he caught, but it was still open and some of the contents spilled into the street.

He stooped to start gathering up the little packets, but a yell and a brandished fist from the larger of the pub goers sent him packing.

"Wow," Emily breathed. "They chased him off? They've not cleaned up their act here now have they?"

"Not likely," Mads said. "I reckon they're trying to keep the old-school drugs out. Guess they prefer Juliana's brand." She paused in thought, "You know, I don't think I've ever heard of anyone ever ODing or anything on her stuff. Is that right Gabe?"

The gargoyle turned slowly to look down at Mads, 'Gabe' didn't seem to sit well with him. "Indeed," he began disdainfully, "Her potions are not bone-fide narcotics. Just a simple energy transfer spell with a little... kicker, to make the imbiber feel a little lightheaded."

"So, if they're still chucking the OG pushers out then that must mean that someone's still supplying Juliana's drugs then?" Mads reasoned.

Emily nodded in the gloom.

"Means we've got to wait it out a little longer." She said.

Emily slumped down with her back to the wall. At least the biting wind was a little less spiteful in the partial shelter.

She glanced back over her shoulder. Gabriel and Mads had gone back to their lookout positions.

"You two okay up there?" she asked.

"Mistress, I have done nothing but stare down from a rooftop for *hundreds* of years; one more night will not be the end of me."

Mads scoffed, "I bet you feel right at home up here then?"

"I have never known what home really is." came the poignant reply.

Emily pulled her backpack towards her and took out a small thermos, poured herself some hot chocolate into the plastic cup.

As she sipped the sweet liquid, it warmed her and her mind drifted to thoughts of warmer times.

The heatwave of 2022 was an inconvenience for a lot of folk in the leafy suburbs of the UK. But in the stifling concrete towers of the city, there was little escape from the raging sun.

No breeze blew through the tower complex where Mads lived with her Dad. The air hung like hot, dry blankets around the block.

They had heeded the advice to keep the curtains drawn, even the windows closed against common intuition. But the heat built up in the small flat. Relentless and maddeningly inescapable.

Mads peered through the curtains, the searing midday light making her squint and grimace. There was no air! No air!

Frantically, she scrambled at the handle to the window and threw it open. A furnace-blast of air swirled in making her gasp and slam it shut again.

"Just leave it, girl." A weak voice from the armchair in the corner of the room.

"Dad, sorry I didn't realise you were awake."

She stepped over to where her father lay, sprawled in the large chair. She took the flannel from a bowl of water by his side, wrung it out and pressed it gently to his forehead. He smiled and shifted in his seat.

"No, just lay back." Mads soothed. "It's time for your pills, I'll go get them."

While Mads clattered about in the kitchen, fetching a glass of iced water, her Father winced in pain as he eased himself out from his seat. He hobbled towards the cluttered desk by the window and began rummaging around.

"Dad, no. You shouldn't be up." She took his arm, but he shrugged her off.

"Just a moment, Princess." He fussed about at the desk, leafing through paperwork, muttering to himself.

Mads picked up the plastic pill organiser and tipped four coloured pills and capsules into her hand.

"Come on, come sit and take these," she urged.

"Cho Man!" Her father muttered under his breath in Jamaican patois. "Where 'dat damn 'ting." Then he finally found what he was looking for and shuffled back to his chair in the corner, clutching a manila envelope.

He sat heavily and cursed again, "Okay, I take you damn pills now."

She passed him the glass. Most of the ice had already melted, and it dripped with condensation.

Mads' phone rang.

"You gon answer dat?" Her Dad looked between her and the mobile buzzing on the arm of the sofa.

"I'm waiting for you to swallow those pills, Dad." Hands on hips, glowering back at him. "Come on Dad, you know you have to."

Reluctantly, he shoved the pills into his mouth and swigged at the cold water.

"Happy now?"

Mads nodded and looked at her phone, it was Emily.

The instant she picked up, she knew something was wrong. A moment too long of silence, then a sniffle.

"I've... Messed it all... Up," came her words through bitter sobs. "All of it."

"Messed– What happened?" Then she remembered. Today was GCSE results day. She had offered to go down to the school with her to collect her results, but Emily had wanted to go alone.

"Oh, shit Em. How bad?"

There was a rustling of paper, "English Lit two, English Lang three, Geography one..." she let out a shuddering sob, "Maths U. Fuck, Mads a U in maths. I've got *nothing*!"

This was a disaster, Mads couldn't believe this. "But you were getting fives and sixes in your mocks before Christmas, those were strong passes. How can..." She couldn't think of anything to say that didn't sound like she was berating her.

"Look, stay there, you're at home, right?"

A mumbled, 'yes'.

"I'm coming over, we can talk things through."

She hung up and saw her father looking at her with a sad expression.

"You can get by in this world without schooling," he said "Jus look at me. Outa school at fifteen, worked hard at my grandfather's business 'till I got the boat here."

"Yeah, I know the story, but things are different now."

"If you work hard, you'll be jus fine. Look at dis place, it's not a lot but it's all mine. No rent to pay." He dropped his eyes for a moment, "Course your poor mother, God rest her, she graft like a horse too."

"There's no way Emily can get any kind of job with no qualifications."

He looked up and into her eyes, "You sweet on dat girl, aren't you?" He smiled, and the expression filled his eyes.

Mads nodded, "I am. Yes, it's true, but—"

"But nuttin' princess. I see she make you happy. If you happy, then the whole world's right."

Mads took a step closer, "You think so?" she whispered, a lump rising in her throat.

"I *know* so. She right for you and right now, she need you. Go. Go make tings right wit' her."

Mads threw her arms around her father and held him, "Oh, Dad. I was so scared that you wouldn't understand. I love you so much."

He coughed and waved her on.

"Don' forget you sunscreen, you burn out dere like toast."

Mads arrived at Emily's door, panting and slick with sweat. She leaned against the door frame with one arm and took a long swig from her water bottle.

The door flew open and Emily hurled herself into a sobbing embrace, dragging the larger girl inside and slamming the door.

Emily's eyes were pink and swollen with crying, much the same colour as Mads' face, shoulders and arms.

She was sticky and hot to the touch as Emily buried her face in her neck and groaned.

"Crap," she gasped, pulling back. "Look at you, you're burned."

"It's brutal out there," Mads panted, "Look at me, I'm never out of breath when I run here. She tugged at her navy lycra and it slapped back wetly.

Emily's eyes widened briefly, but she pushed it back.

"Come in," she said simply, and led her to the kitchen.

Mads sat the empty glass down on the counter and looked Emily directly in the eye.

"What's done is done now," she said levelly. "You can retake next year, even do your GCSEs over again. You'll ace it."

Emily leaned back against the worktop and shook her head. "No, I'm done with all this. I can't go back to that place – not ever."

"Look, if those scumbags are the real reason you want to give up, just think what chance there is of those fuckheads coming back next year for A-Levels." She picked up the glass and drained the last few drops from the bottom, "You're not going to see those idiots ever again," she scoffed. "Well, unless you're getting a burger or something."

"Shit, Mads you think I've even got a chance

flipping burgers now?" She ran her hands through her hair, tugging at it in frustration, "I don't know what to do now. And—" she halted, fear washing over her pale face, "... and when my parents find out I fucked up..." she trailed off, lip quivering and fresh tears rolling down her cheeks.

Mads stepped across the kitchen and held her until the sobbing had subsided. She smoothed her hair and whispered reassuring words to her "Don't worry, I'll look after you my love," she found herself saying.

Emily looked up into her eyes and whispered "You will?"

It was at that point that Madelene Bailey's heart melted and she fully realised that it was true. "Forever," she whispered back, trembling.

Her – strong Madeline – trembling, wanting to dissolve into tears of... this was something new, something that was looming like a tidal wave ready to engulf her and sweep her away like scraps of palm leaf on the white beaches she remembered as a girl when her mother was still alive.

Emily pulled her head down towards her and she was powerless to resist as she kissed her softly and deeply with a passion and assertiveness that made her gasp at first, then simply melt into her embraces like warm butter.

She was only partly aware that Emily had peeled away and was pulling her by the hand, out of the kitchen and towards the stairs.

On the kitchen counter, abandoned, Emily's phone began to buzz.

The mid-afternoon heat and sheer exhaustion won in the end. Flushed and soaked with perspiration, the two young women basked in the glorious breeze from the overhead fan as it quietly circled Emily's war-torn bed.

If sex had ever been described as cathartic, then this was the very definition. Not only was her gasping release a vent for her pent-up frustration, but the reassurance that Mads was there for her was like the weight of the world had been taken from her shoulders. She felt light, she could breathe, despite the heavy, cloying atmosphere.

A little cooler, but no less driven by the burning fire within, they resumed with renewed vigour.

A solid half-hour later both received the shock of their lives. Something that neither of them had expected but had made Mads squeal with surprise, and excitement. It had only been a tiny, clumpy spit, but it had almost hit her in the eye. Recoiling, startled she fell off the edge of the bed. Emily leaned over to find her wiping the cloudy fluid from her face and they had collapsed into laughter.

"It's never done *that* before," Emily managed, through uncontrollable laughter.

"...you not hear me call? They closed the office because of the— what the BLUE BLAZES!"

Emily's Dad was standing in the doorway, fists balled, shaking with rage.

Like scared rabbits, the pair darted and scrambled to retrieve a sheet, a pillow, anything that had been thrown about the room in a futile attempt to cover themselves.

Emily had scuttled into the corner of the room wrapped in the thin summer sheet that had been tossed carelessly to the floor earlier, she whimpered and tried to make herself smaller.

Mads had grabbed a couple of pillows and found herself crouched behind the bed where she had fallen.

"HOW DARE you defile my daughter under MY roof!" Emily's Dad raged.

This burst the bubble of fear that Mads was caught in. *Defile?* Slowly, she unfolded and stood, then dropped the pillows, standing defiantly naked before the beet-faced man.

"I should beat you to within an inch—" he growled.

Mads took a step forward, taught muscles rolling under her creamy white skin.

Emily's Dad jumped back, pointing a shaking finger, "You. You put on some clothes right now, Girl. Just look at yourself." He turned his head to one side, embarrassed, or frightened to look her in the eye.

Coolly, Mads retrieved the two abandoned scraps of Lycra from the floor, gracefully stepped into the pants and slipped the halter-top over her head, adjusting the fit in complete silence.

"Is that it? That's hardly any better."

"It's all I have." Mads said in a low voice, still standing firm. She turned her head towards where Emily had buried herself, her terrified eyes just about visible through a gap in the sheets.

She extended her arm towards her, "Em?"

"Get – out – of – my – house!" came the strangled cry from Emily's Dad.

Mads looked from him to Emily.

"Now! Before I call the police."

"It's okay... I'll talk with you later," a tiny voice from the corner.

Mads fixed Emily's Dad with a stare and marched past him, down the stairs, slamming the door on her way out.

It was only now that Emily saw the crumpled sheet of paper in her father's trembling fist. Fear washed through her afresh in an elevator-drop sensation that almost made her gag.

She stumbled to her feet, wrapped in the sunny yellow sheet, "Dad, I—"

"Don't you speak. You listen to me." He brandished the paper causing Emily to step back and fall to sit on the edge of the bed. She knew this was her exam results, he must have picked it up in the kitchen.

"What do you think you have been doing this last two years? Every. Single. One. Of your exams, FAILED!" He punctuated his words by thrusting the paper towards Emily, she flinched at each.

"They're not all—" she attempted.

"A three, your best score," he snarled with venom in his voice. "And now I see why you've thrown it all away." He waved the tattered scrap behind him towards the stairs, "You've been led astray by that *girl*." He spat the final word, quite literally. A fleck of saliva flew from his mouth. "Get dressed."

Emily shuffled, "Dad. Do you mind?" She said, looking to the door behind him.

He stood his ground, but turned his back to her. "Very well."

Clutching the sheet, Emily gathered up her clothes

from around the room. Her panties hung over the door where they had landed when Mads twirled them around her finger and flung them behind her. Emily had to push past her Dad to retrieve them. He hurrumphed sourly.

"I'm done," she declared quietly once she had dressed.

He turned, and appraised her in her black shorts, black *Rising Dead* t-shirt.

"Good God, look at you," he breathed. "Is it any wonder, you let that sick girl take advantage of you in that way. My God, I wish we'd had you *fixed* when you were a baby. Now..." He threw the paper to the ground.

"But Dad, this is who I am. *What* I am. I don't need *fixing!*"

"So? That's that then is it? You're just going to throw away everything that your mother and I have done for you for the last sixteen years?"

"But I can't help it, Mads and I—"

"What? Mads and you, what? You're in *love*? Is that what you want to say to me?" He put his hands to his temples and roared.

"It's WRONG Emily, what you're doing, what you've done. It doesn't matter that she hardly looks like a girl, good God, you're hardly a girl yourself." He thrust an accusatory hand in the direction of her baggy black shorts.

At that, Emily burst into hot tears and fled the room.

"Go then! Go be with your *girlfriend*." Emily's footsteps thundered down the stairs. "Don't expect to come back to this house," he yelled after her as the door slammed shut.

The run back to her flat was brutal in the afternoon heat. Mads didn't feel up to being around people, even an air-conditioned bus wasn't enough to tempt her.

The stink from the bins outside the stairwell was appalling, and the stairs up to her floor were worse than ever.

Hot, sticky and thoroughly hacked off with the bigots of the world, she shut the door to the flat and leaned against it as if to keep the world outside from getting in.

At least the flat was quiet. She looked over to the continuance of that silence in her dad's armchair.

The next morning, Mads slit open the envelope she found resting in her father's lap. His will left her the flat, its contents and a modest savings account.

CHAPTER 12

UK LAW DICTATED that the pub should stop serving drinks and close up at eleven. Of course, the law was taken with a rather liberal pinch of salt around these parts.

Even so, as the time dragged towards midnight and the most persistent hangers-on had stumbled noisily down the street, Emily grew to feel that it was futile to wait any longer.

They had seen nothing of interest after the rookie dealer was given his marching orders.

"We should go." Emily said through gritted teeth which were beginning to chatter. The hot chocolate had long since gone cold and tiny twinkles on the gravelled and mossy roofing felt heralded the start of a wicked frost.

Mads flipped over and sat up. "You're right. There's no sign here at all is there? Maybe we ought to go check out where she lives. See if she's holed up there?"

"You're seriously suggesting that we go visit a *witch's house at midnight?*" Emily scoffed.

"Aw, come on. It'll be fine. If she's not already dead, she's done for."

"Your miting speaks the truth dear mistress," Gabriel fawned.

"Okay then Gabe," Mads cried cheerfully, "Lead on." She slapped his rump. He rolled his eyes and scuttled over the parapet like a bloated lizard.

"See you at the bottom – wheee..." Mads hurled herself over the edge.

Emily sighed and trudged over to where the ladder rails looped up over the side of the building. The metal was icy cold and bit into her hands as she gingerly climbed down the rusting metalwork.

She emerged from the dark of the alley like something from a horror movie; all long black hair and menacing scowl. "Come on then, let's go," she grumbled. "Is it far?"

"No mistress," Gabriel chirped, "It's just this way. Ten minutes if you walk like that."

With a cackle, he bounded off towards where Emily remembered a dilapidated row of townhouses stood. Gabriel leapt cat-like over one of the concrete rings, but in his enthusiasm, misjudged and clipped his undercarriage on the edge with a flash of orange sparks and gritty projectiles.

Emily trudged along after him with Mads hopping merrily beside her.

Perhaps once, this short street was something rather grand, but half the street lights were out and if there were once houses on the right hand side of the street, they had been pulled down years ago and the land left derelict and undeveloped.

The residences on the remaining side looked like they might fall down before they were pulled down. Of the maybe two dozen houses on the row, Emily guessed that only a handful were still occupied.

Trash lay in the street – there were no cars parked there and other, bulky items were left to rot on the steps leading up to most of the boarded up or graffitied doors.

"This one." Gabriel indicated a door. Black painted and strong looking. Perhaps the only one on the street that wouldn't burst into rotten splinters with a good kick.

The windows looked sound, and the only way to the back was round the entire block.

Gabriel saw Emily eyeing the door doubtfully.

"Wait," he called and scaled the building in a flash, clattering across the loose roof tiles, over the top and out of sight.

Emily waited in the cold and dark. The wind whipped around her in a cruel gust that made her pull her jacket in closer.

A noise at the door made her step back and nearly trip on what she hoped was just a soggy cardboard box. Bolts slid and clunked inside then Gabriel gurned around the door as it opened soundlessly.

"Ladies; if you please." He bowed and held the door open like a tiny, creepy butler.

Emily fished a little torch out of her bag before entering, glancing nervously down the street. It looked empty, but the shadows there could easily have hidden anyone or anything.

It was darker inside though. Pitch dark.

"Are you sure those two weird bodyguards aren't in there?" she whispered.

"Certain. Those two zombies would never have found their way back here after the... Incident in the alley. Likely, they wandered off like lost sheep and fell in the canal."

"Zombies?" Emily whispered, peering in, straining her eyes, "For real? Like in *The Rising Flesh*?"

"Oh, their flesh is risen for sure, mistress. But be at peace, they aren't inside here."

Emily stepped inside uncertainly and jumped as Gabriel closed the door plunging her into total darkness.

"*It's okay,*" Mads sent. "*I can see pretty well, it's clear.*"

Emily remembered the torch and switched it on; the powerful white beam hit Gabriel full in the face; he hissed and slunk into the shadow.

"*Look, let's stick to the farsight, psychic thingy for now. If those two are here, we don't want to alert them.*"

"*Trust me, if they were here, you'd know about it.*" Gabriel sent.

The old house must easily have been over a

hundred years old, and by the looks of it hadn't been redecorated since it was built.

"It's clean, I'll give her that," Mads sent. *"I mean, this is a witches house after all – where are all the cobwebs and thick dust?*

"Those two zombies must be handy with a duster," Mads sent, chuckling.

"Those two shambling corpses wouldn't know a duster from a doorknob." Gabriel cut in with a slightly hurt expression, *"For decades, I've tended this accursed place."*

Mads looked up at Emily with an expression of surprise. It would be hard for either of them to get the image of this ugly stone brute busying himself about the house cleaning and dusting. They decided to let it go, lest they upset him.

"Um, you did a nice job." Emily settled for.

"The mi- The witch's chambers are at the top of the house." Gabriel advised without acknowledgement.

Carefully, they made their way up the uncarpeted stairs. They were painted or lacquered black or incredibly dark brown and would be treacherous to walk back down.

Emily had expected to see old, creepy photos or paintings along the walls up the stairs, but they were bare except for some kind of striped, maybe velvet wallpaper.

"She has no family here." Gabriel sent as if he sensed what she was thinking. *"None living, at least."*

Emily shone her torch upwards, it caught his face leering between the ornate stair-rods.

"She's Jamacan, isn't she? Like my Dad. I can tell

from the way she talks." Mads sent. She was a little ahead of Emily, on the next floor now with Gabriel.

"*She came on a boat from Jamaica.*"

"*Yeah, same thing. Dad came over in 1970. Just a tiny baby. I think my grandparents were the last of the Windrush immigrants or something like that. Was she the same?*"

"*No,*" the gargoyle said brusquely, "*She came over before that.*" He shuffled off along the threadbare carpet and thudded up the next flight of stairs.

"*Why does she need a big house like this just for herself?*" Emily asked. The landing was narrow, but it was long. There were two doors, she opened one and shone her torch inside.

It was completely empty. Bare floorboards, no furniture, just heavy curtains covering the window that looked out onto the street below.

"I guess it's the same in all the other rooms," she muttered to herself.

At the top of the stairs was a single door. Gabriel was waiting beside it for Emily.

"*Her chambers,*" he sent silently.

Emily took a breath and readied herself for what might be inside. She would settle very nicely for a withered corpse – not something she had ever imagined in her life wishing for, but times change.

Gabriel opened the door suddenly and barrelled inside, Emily followed as soon as she realised what was happening, followed by Mads.

Her torch swung about wildly, picking out shapes and shadows. The room seemed huge. She could hear Mads running about, but the sound of her tiny feet was too much like some kind of rodent scurrying about in the blackness – it creeped her out badly.

Eventually, the beam of the torch swept across what looked like a bed – a four-poster, complete with curtains. Drawn of course.

Her heart was racing now, thumping in her chest. If there was anywhere that the witch would be, dead or alive, this would surely be it.

"Is she in there?" Emily whispered, forgetting herself and breaking the silence. Well, they'd made enough noise bursting into the room, so no point sneaking about now.

She lunged for the bed and flung the curtains wide, aiming the light inside. Fury burning behind her eyes, building to a white-hot blinding flash that tore the curtains from their wooden poles and sent them fluttering to the ground.

The bed was empty.

"Holy shit Em!" Mads yelled, hopping up onto the vast antique bed.

Emily was doubled over with her hands on her knees panting. She looked up and saw the glinting black eyes in the light of the small torch that had dropped onto the musty blankets.

"Not here," Emily gasped.

Mads took a step forwards, "No. But THAT. Just do that again when we find her and she'll be history."

Gabriel emerged from the shadows, "Truly impressive Mistress." He stroked his little mossy soul-patch, "Such *power*."

Emily sat on the edge of the bed, her breathing was beginning to return to normal. Mads jumped into her lap.

"So, what now? Where is she? Is she even alive still?"

"She lives still, I am sure of it. She is old and wise, and cunning. I know of a place where she would go should she be truly close to her end. A hidden place."

"Where?" said Emily, "I'm ready to finish this."

Mads snuggled into her lap, "My hero," she joked.

"An infirmaria. Long abandoned and forgotten."

"Inferma- what?" Mads asked.

"A hospital. The old hospital. We passed it on the way to see Kelley. I know where that is."

Emily rummaged in her bag and pulled out her phone. The screen briefly lit up her face, then shut off.

"But we've got to go home first."

"How come?" Mads asked.

"Low battery, I'm not falling into that old trap of getting stuck at the bottom of some flooded lift shaft with no phone battery."

Mads nodded sagely.

"Plus, screw all this midnight witch-hunt shit. We're going in the morning when it's light."

"Okay, Cab's going to be here in ten minutes," Emily said. "You want to ride in the bag or on the chain?"

"In the bag, I think. It makes me dizzy spinning about like that." She looked up at Emily, "Are you sure about this? What we talked about after Gabriel set off?"

Emily nodded. "As sure as I can be. We've got to end this, get you back."

The cab set them down at the same drop-off point as before. Emily thought it might seem a bit strange if the cab took her out to the derelict part of the hospital. Even stranger had she been carrying a stone gargoyle with her. Gabriel had set off just before dawn under the cover of darkness, leaving specific instructions on where to meet.

It wasn't a long walk. The gap in the chain-link fence was where Gabriel said it would be. Broken glass crunched under Emily's boots on the moss patched piece of tar-mac outside the old hospital entrance.

The frost from the night before had thawed, and it wasn't as cold as yesterday, but the wind still whipped around Emily as she made her way uncertainly towards the derelict building. Most of the windows were broken and pieces of trim were hanging and swinging dangerously in the wind.

A flock – no, a *murder* – of crows erupted from somewhere behind the main building, making Emily gasp and look up as they circled and called to each other. Some settled back on a red-brick chimney from which a delicate curl of dark smoke rode away on the gusting wind. She shuddered and pulled her coat tight.

The main doors were boarded up tightly as Gabriel had told them. Around the corner, the side-door was propped open with a broken brick.

"He described this place very well," Mads said climbing out from Emily's bag and dropping to the floor. "Where *is* the little git then?"

Emily pulled the door open and peered inside. It was dark, and no sign of Gabriel.

"You think we should just go in?" Emily asked, her voice echoing coldly.

"You fancy hanging about in this weather?" Mads asked, "If the cold doesn't kill you something's likely to drop on you." As she spoke, a gust blew up and rattled something metallic sounding above them.

Emily looked up aprehensively and ducked inside, Mads quickly followed.

"The bri—" Mads shouted, but the wind caught the door and without the makeshift doorstop, slammed shut behind them with a crash that reverberated down the dark passageway.

Emily cursed and fished the torch out of her bag. The metal release bar to the emergency exit they had just come through was missing and the mechanism wrecked.

"Okay, well it looks like we're in then," Mads said. "But that bloody gargoyle's stood us up. We've no idea where we're going!"

"Yes. We do." Emily grinned to herself, "I know exactly where she is."

Mads trotted ahead of her and stopped, looking up. "Where? How on Earth can you possibly know? This place is huge."

"She's in the basement, the old boiler room to be exact."

Mads threw her arms up in the air, "I mean, sure, the basement's about the spookiest place you can get here... apart from the morgue, so that makes sense."

"If this place is closed down, then how come there's smoke coming from one of the chimneys?"

Mads nodded her head, impressed. "Figures."

Emily shone the torch down the corridor which defiantly swallowed the light; it could have gone on forever. The impenetrable blackness filled her with dread. Either side of the corridor, rows of closed doors could have contained any number of horrors.

A shiver ran down Emily's spine, "We should make a move."

Slowly, they made their way down the corridor. Emily made the mistake of looking behind her and seeing that the door they had entered through had been engulfed by the dark. In front and behind was now a fathomless abyss of black with them in a tiny bubble of light.

To her relief, a door at the end soon resolved itself from the fog-like blackness and they pushed through it from the cloying, claustrophobic passage... Into a much larger space.

To the left, must have been the entrance, where gaps and breaks in the boarding had let in a little of the grey January light. It was just enough to make out the vaguest of shapes here. It seemed that this was a main corridor which ran through the old hospital; it was wide and stretched off to the right into pitch blackness.

Emily's heavy boots clumped and reverberated in the large, empty space and she imagined other sounds joining the echoes as they washed back over from the unseen depths.

"Look, a sign." Mads said. Her voice sounded out of place, coming as it did from inside her head, rather than through the darkness. It still had warmth to it. This place sucked all the life out of everything. Every sound was harsh and cold, the gloom took away any colour. So, as Emily shone her torch up at the large panel, the brightly coloured stripes denoting various departments seemed suddenly alien.

"Hmm. All medical departments. They're not really going to have any signs to the boiler room are they," she whispered.

"So, we just try to head down then?"

"I guess. Look, it says lifts and stairs are this way." She pointed her torch uselessly down the passage. It caught an assortment of discarded items; a hospital bed, some boxes against the walls.

The wind outside made a low moan through the gaps as they headed towards the lift lobby.

It wasn't far, but of course felt so much further when the way ahead was so uncertain.

There were lifts to both sides of the corridor here, which had widened out into a large atrium. Above, walkways led away to unknown depths.

There were two doors leading to stairs, presumably to a matching area below. Emily pushed the door open to yet more blackness. It was beginning to grate on her nerves.

Suddenly, a sound.

The shock washed through Emily, icy cold and she stopped, halfway through the door hardly daring to breathe. It took a second for Emily's brain to process what the sound was past the initial lizard-brain reaction to the crash from below. It sounded like someone had dropped a metal tray somewhere in the distance.

Mads swore in Emily's head and rushed to the metal

stair railings to look over.

"Be careful," Emily rasped.

"Someone's down there."

"It might be Gabriel, or the wind, or... or just this old place falling to bits," Mads replied hopefully, but she didn't sound particularly convincing.

"We should have brought a weapon of some sort." Mads looked up imploringly. "We have no idea what we're up against here."

"I'll look for something." She took a deep breath and started down the concrete steps, holding tightly to the rail as she descended.

The doorway at the landing below opened up onto what seemed like another public area of the hospital, so they ventured deeper.

There were no further sounds, save for her slow footsteps and breath, which she fought to keep slow and even.

This was now the bottom of the steps, which meant that on one hand, they need not go any deeper, but on the other, they were likely closer to where they heard the crash... and whatever made it.

Switching off the torch, Emily pushed her ear against the door. No sound.

Slowly, carefully she opened it and leaned through. No lights.

She switched on the torch and yelped. Just a tall cage trolley piled with odds and ends parked in front of the door.

"Shit, Mads you could have warned me," she Growled.

"Sorry, sorry, sorry," she cried, running between her

legs and into the passageway.

This was different from the floor above, it didn't look like the areas that patients would normally go. Using her enhanced vision, Mads could see that there were boxes and trollies crammed all along the passage. Old medical equipment and supplies – broken, abandoned waiting for someone else to deal with.

"Looks clear," she advised, "Just a ton of junk, watch your step."

"Let's see if there's anything here I can use if things get tricky," Emily breathed. She shone the torch over the tall trollies nearest her. They were stacked with mattresses, pillows, bedding. Further down the row, some kind of medical equipment; monitors or something. They looked antique with their old-style screens.

"What about this?" Mads pointed to a metal stand, the kind that bags of blood or drips were hung from. The metal pole looked like it was in sections. Perhaps she could separate it, swing it at an assailant?

A large plastic storage box next to it caught Emily's eye. The top came off with an annoyingly loud popping sound; her eyes widened and she drew a slow breath.

"Bingo!" she whispered excitedly.

The box was crammed full of wicked looking surgical tools, clamps, a nasty looking hammer, what appeared to be a drill for heaven's sake, and...

"This." Said Emily, carefully pulling out a horrifying saw-like blade. "Oh, please let there be another." Carefully, she pushed aside the discarded tools, taking out a couple of the larger items to make it easier to search, then giggled in delight when she extracted the twin implement she was looking for.

"Look!" She held out the two vicious, items to her sides.

Mads picked the torch up off the floor and shone it towards Emily.

"Oh, fucking Ho! *Bonesaws*, Em! You look just like Michelle from *Rising Flesh!*"

"Too fucking right." She gave them an experimental swing and reflections from the surgical steel flashed in the torchlight.

"Let's go, you carry the torch."

Buoyed with the confidence of now being able to defend herself – heroically even, they moved down the dark passageway at a better pace. It rounded a corner and then ended in a larger, square space, empty of junk.

To the right, a large lift door, and opposite a pair of swing doors.

"Doesn't look like the entrance to the plant-room to me," Emily whispered. "We'll check, though yeah?"

Holding both her weapons in one hand, she pushed one of the heavy doors open and felt the blood drain from her face.

Stepping inside, she was faced with a wall of stainless steel drawers.

They were in the morgue.

She shivered, "Thank fuck it's empty."

Mads turned to shine the torch back on the doors so they could leave this ghastly place. The beam swung across a dark figure in the corner of the room.

Emily caught a gasp in her throat and Mads instinctively flicked the torch back.

Standing motionless facing the corner of the room was one of Juliana's guards.

Emily began to whimper and edge towards the door, Mads kept the torch trained on it – if she lost sight of it in this darkness even she wouldn't know where it was if it moved. And yet it still stood inert, back to them in the corner.

They were just at the door now. Emily reached out to gently push it open when one of the knives slipped from her hand and crashed to the floor.

The zombie stiffened and turned, soundlessly locking them in its dead gaze. In that instant, Emily swept Mads up, still clutching the torch and barrelled through the door, a scream finally making its way from her searing lungs to her throat.

The only way out was back the way they came through the chicanery of boxes and cage trollies. Emily pushed one aside but a loose sheet tangled itself around her shins and brought her to a painful thud on the dusty floor.

Both Mads and the torch went sliding in front of her as her hands slapped against the worn linoleum. She hit her face and yelled from the pain, fear and frustration.

Franticly, in the dark she kicked at the sheet which seemed to have become even more tightly wound around her legs.

Mads scrambled for the little pen-torch and darted back to illuminate the scene. The beam flicked up to the black beyond Emily's tied feet and even she with her human vision caught movement of the zombie rounding the corner. The shock at how quickly it was moving ignited a fresh spark of panic, but before she could untie herself, it was all but upon her.

The saw.

It lay just to her side, *why hadn't she picked it up earlier*. Dragging herself backwards by her elbows, she grabbed the weapon and lashed out. The blade slashed at the Zombie's calf and it lurched to the side, tripping and sliding on other sheets that had spilled out of the cage. Emily had half expected for the leg to fly cleanly off and land with a wet thud across the passage. It was a horrifying gash, but they *lie* on TV, she realised.

With a yell, Mads dropped the torch which spun wildly on the floor, illuminating the scene in a rapidly rotating strobe. She leapt up and onto the back of the Zombie, clinging tightly to the collar of the expensive suit it wore.

The creature was distracted for long enough to allow Emily to begin work again on her trapped legs.

Mads tried to bleed away whatever life-force that might be within the apparition, but rather then a nourishing golden mist, a sickly yellow-green vapour poured out. It made Mads choke and dropped off like a cigarette-burned leach.

Emily pulled one last time and freed her legs. Scrambling up the side of the trolley, she shoved the heavy cage over onto its side. It fell with a deafening crash and as it did, spilled the remaining contents out onto the floor just in front of the flailing corpse. The fallen trolley, being just as high as Emily herself all but filled the width of the passage and made a sturdy waist-high barricade.

Bereft of human sense, the zombie crawled directly towards Emily, but in its confusion had found itself trapped inside the metal framework and grasped in numb futility with its bony fingers.

A small, dark shape leapt from behind the blockade – it was Mads. She quickly regained control of the torch. *"Go! Let's GO!"* she yelled silently.

Emily came to her senses and staggered backwards into a pile of boxes which scattered their contents on the floor. She turned while Mads scaled her backpack and clung onto the strap, shining the torch over her shoulder to guide the way.

Racing headlong into the darkness, Emily dodged the maze of obstacles until they were almost upon the entrance to the stairwell.

The second zombie stepped silently out of the shadow.

Adrenaline and primal instinct fed by too many comics and TV shows were on Emily's side this time. With a startled gasp, she planted the bone-saw square in the forehead of the monster before it even had time to react.

It slumped down against the door with a gurgle then fell wedging it half open.

"Shit, Em! That was wicked." Mads crowed from her shoulder.

Emily paused, bent double, with her hands on her knees to catch her breath. "Just like in the comic!" She panted. "I think Jake Mayer just saved my life."

"Looks like he was right all along then." Mads said.

She swung the torch about while Emily composed herself.

It was quiet now, no movement in the shadows. Well, apart from...

"You know you've got to do it." She said sombrely. "It's a dumb fuck, but if it *does* get free we're going to have more trouble."

"I know, I know." She marched back to the fallen trolley where Juliana's henchman raved and snarled.

A swift flash of steel through a gap in the bars and the thing was silent.

CHAPTER 13

THERE REALLY WASN'T much point in going back up the stairs to the ground level. The best option was to continue along the passageway in the direction they had yet to explore.

"Should we move him?" Mads asked.

"No, he's not doing any harm propping the door open." She glanced down at the twice-dead corpse and grimaced. "Besides, he's super-gross. I don't wanna touch him."

They reached a t-junction after maybe thirty metres and at last, luck was with them. A red sign with white letters indicated that the boiler room was to their left.

"I see a big door at the end!" Mads said excitedly. "That *has* to be it."

Emily let out a long breath, "I still don't know what to expect though. I wish Gabriel was here to help."

"To hell with him; we just get in there, kill the old hag and leg it – simple."

"Just how old is this place?" Emily murmured. She had stopped below an air vent which had its metal grilles bent and twisted by what looked like tree roots. They appeared to have spewed out and spread along the ceiling, searching for moisture and sustenance.

"There's more here." Mads pointed to another root-bound vent.

"It must be the..." Emily trailed off, uncertainly, "Sorry. Er, the... What was I saying?"

There was no answer because Mads was laying face down on the dirty floor.

"You didn' even haff dinner." Emily mumbled, "Ifsh... If..." and she too slowly collapsed to the ground. As consciousness faded, she thought she saw the roots on the ceiling writhe and move.

How much time had passed? Emily had no way of telling. She felt as if she were in the most comfortable bed, she had just eaten a sumptuous feast, and maybe more than a glass or two of delicious wine. It was a glorious feeling and she could happily just lounge all day in these satin sheets, her head on pillows made from clouds themselves.

If it weren't for that annoying... that annoying... Oh never mind, it didn't matter. Was there something tugging at her foot? No, she must have dreamed it.

Oh, there was music now. Soft, gentle waves of sound, like the lapping of cool water at the edge of a lake on a warm summer's day. A familiar scent drifted towards her, she was in her own private tropical paradise. Maybe she should—

Owch! A needle-prick to her ear. How rude of whoever it was to disturb her peace, this really was—

"Shit!" Emily snapped her eyes open and tried to swat whatever it was that had nipped her ear, but she couldn't move her arm, her legs, she was trapped!

A shiny black snout sniffed at her face, whiskers brushed her cheek, then a flash of orange and it was gone.

"What the fuck?" Emily groaned. Her senses were beginning to pour back in now. The warm embrace she had felt earlier became the crush and pinch of roots, flooding down from the ceiling, wrapping themselves around her and she presumed also Mads.

Faint golden wisps dissolved into the air as she struggled against her bonds.

As she pushed, they creaked and began to make sharp splitting sounds. Tiny puffs of gold escaped and vanished from fractures in the roots as they tore away from her.

Those that had let out their life force, quickly became brittle and shattered as Emily thrashed.

"Mads! Mads! Wake up, it's a trap! She's trying to drain you!"

"I'm stuck!" Came the reply. Not muffled of course, but as she pulled herself up onto one elbow, she could see a knot of smaller rootlets pulsating.

Kicking away the last of the splintering tendrils, Emily grasped the tangle and tugged it away from the larger, feed-roots. It quickly dried up and crumbled, then burst apart as Mads recovered her senses and fought back.

Behind her, a skitter of claws made her spin her head around. In the remaining light of the fading torch, the outline of a fox stopped to look back at her momentarily then vanished silently around the corner.

"Oh my God!" Mads sobbed. "How long have we been stuck like this?"

The torch was laying underneath a heap of gnarled root pieces. Emily grabbed it and shone it about.

The little LED penlight had started the day fully charged with a blinding white beam. Now, it had diminished to a sickly grey light.

"It must have been hours, Mads." Emily said, with a shiver. "I hardly ever need to charge this."

"You've got your little power bank?" Mads asked, glancing at the backpack.

"Yeah, but let's save that if I need it for my phone. We can manage."

"But this totally proves we're on the right track, she has to b—"

The door at the end of the corridor slowly began to open. Both girls gasped and looked towards the creaking sound.

"Gabriel?" Mads asked, peering ahead.

"I have languished on a ledge for a hundred years, but that is nothing to the wait for you. You dally and wander like lost souls. The day is gone now. Hurry, the witch lies within." He turned on his heel and vanished back inside, letting the heavy door slam behind him.

Mads and Emily looked at each other for a second or two in disbelief.

"What was that all about?" Mads asked.

"Honestly, I have no idea. But look, he's found her and he's fine – so she has to be really weak or she would have attacked him, right?"

"Guess so." They started towards the large plant-room doors. "I bet that root trap thing must have taken a lot out of her."

"Did you see that fox just now? It must have wandered in. It was nibbling at my bloody ear while I was out." She rubbed it and looked at her hand. There wasn't any blood. "It was a good job that door was propped open though." She said as an afterthought. "I don't think I would have woken up otherwise."

The plant room was large and full of shapes and shadows of equipment, machinery, boxes and barrels.

There was light.

A fire had been lit in one of the furnaces. The iron door was open and orange flames flickered inside casting a fan of light across the room.

In front of that there was a workbench which seemed to have been pushed away from another near the door.

Emily crept into the room, round the bench, stepping over discarded tools and metal junk.

Gabriel hopped up onto the bench in front of her, grinning in the firelight. Emily looked around the room, the open oven.

"Makes me think of the tale of Hansel and Gretel."

"Yeah, just shove the old witch in there and be done with her," Mads added.

"So, where is she then?"

Gabriel extended a hand, stuck out a clawed finger and pointed it upwards. Two pairs of eyes followed the point to the high ceiling above them.

"Fuck!" Emily leapt backwards in shock, bumping into the bench behind her.

Deep in the shadows of the girders and pipes, a cocoon, or maybe a mummy hung. Threads and straps of translucent material bound her in place, glistening moistly in the shifting light from the fire below.

Like the black head of some ghastly maggot, the grey-skinned face of the witch Juliana protruded from one end.

Her eyes were closed and her bony face crossed with several thin threads of... Emily couldn't imagine what it was.

"We have her." Gabriel said quietly.

Above him, Juliana's eyes slowly opened; the lids pulling stickily apart, then flickered weakly.

"Quick, she's waking up!" Emily cried.

"Give me the knife, I'll climb up and cut her down. But you have to finish her."

Emily shuddered, took a step forward then stopped.

"Em, you've *got* to do it," Mads implored.

Juliana's yellow eyes swivelled around to fix on Emily and her mouth began to open. Blackened and broken teeth revealed behind the crusted lips.

Emily darted forward and handed the bone saw to the gargoyle. From above, a short, wet gurgling rasp drifted down, followed by another building up into a sickly cackle.

"Yes, my mistress," Gabriel hissed slyly, "*we have*

her."

"Gabriel! Quick! Cut her down, she's waking up!" Emily shouted. Mads climbed up to Emily's shoulder making worried sounds.

"Em. Something's not right."

"Cut her down!" Emily repeated, feeling the *power* begin to rise in her. "You're bound to me you have to."

"No." He replied simply and tossed the bone saw behind him into the darkness. He cackled wickedly and snapped his fingers. A tiny golden puff drifted from his hands – the same as had appeared when Emily had bound him. "Poof."

"You're– You're *not* bound to me are you?"

He chuckled again, "Of course not, fool. How else could I deliver the power that my mistress needs to be restored? This much needs a human soul to anchor to, not a vessel of rock." He rapped his head loudly with a knuckle. "Well, that's not entirely true." He reached out for an object on the bench beside him and held it out. It sparkled green in the firelight.

"A power crystal. Pretty, yes?"

Without warning, Juliana's eyes shone with a blinding light and a beam blasted out into the crystal which Gabriel held aloft. The beam seemed to magnify and hit Mads and Emily square on.

With a sound like the air tearing apart, life power blasted back along the beam and into the crystal. The two were locked in place in unimaginable agony as the life was drained from them and captured.

Abruptly, the light ceased and Emily dropped to the ground. Mads rolled onto the floor then slowly picked herself up and staggered back to Emily.

Juliana's head sagged down from her bonds, her eyes closed.

"You deceitful little shit!" Mads bellowed, "You were just fattening us up!"

Emily groaned and shifted slightly. She could see Juliana hanging, exhausted from the ceiling. A small laugh escaped, "Look though. It hasn't worked."

"She's too weak to feed." Gabriel spat with contempt. "Because of *you*."

Emily struggled to her knees and scooped up Mads. She felt limp in her hands and held her tightly to her chest. "Just look, she's nearly dead now."

Gabriel glanced up and in that moment Emily hobbled towards the door to make her escape.

"Not. Dead." Came a voice as dry as paper, then a searing blast hit Emily in the back. She fell headlong behind the bench, dropping Mads.

Gabriel got up onto his hind legs to try to see where they had ended up but they had fallen out of sight. A faint groan came from behind the bench.

"I could have finished them, my mistress," he muttered to the near corpse above. "Don't waste what little life you have. Let me finish them, then you can take all the time you need to feed. Slowly, from this." He placed the crystal carefully onto the bench where he stood and climbed down to the floor.

"No..." Juliana croaked, barely a whisper now, "Leave her for me. Bind her... I will take her myself, such a sweet, sweet delight... the life force of a supernatural." She rasped and coughed then was silent.

He looked about and spotted a length of wire, grabbed it and stared over to where Emily had fallen.

As he did, Emily rose up from behind the bench, her face was cut and her jacket torn. She stepped out revealing a length of broken metal pipe in one hand, jagged and deadly. In the other, Mads hung limp and lifeless, one leg hanging by a thread, stuffing spilling from one side.

"I'm going to smash you to rubble, you granite *gimp*."

He took a step back and looked anxiously up at the motionless wreck. "Mistress. Strike her, strike her!" He pleaded.

The best she could do now was a ragged groan. She had spent next to the last of her energy.

Emily advanced on the repugnant creature as he backed up, "Sweet Emily, I give myself in servitude to y—"

"Not this time, no."

The gargoyle threw himself at her and hit her like the rock that he was. It knocked the breath out of her and she landed on her back, dropping both the pipe and the inert Mads.

Like a flash, he grabbed Mads from the floor and tossed her into the mouth of the furnace.

Emily shrieked, but the pain in her back stopped her from getting up.

"Your poppet is no more now! It's over." He picked up the length of wire and advanced on Emily. Behind him there was a pop and a gout of fire briefly erupted from the furnace.

He grinned again, all sharp teeth – a forked tongue

flicked over his lips as he stooped down to tie Emily's legs.

"I told you," he hissed, "I'm not granite."

"Sedimentary SHITHEAD then, fucker!" It was Mads. Standing on the bench beneath Juliana, holding the crystal above her head.

Gabriel spun on his heels in shock, mouth slack eyes swivelling from Mads to the furnace. "How?" Was all he could manage before the heavy steel pipe that Emily swung at him slammed into his side.

The gargoyle shattered into two large pieces, the top half of his body landing two or three paces from the legs which twitched and thrashed before laying still.

Juliana woke above and began to hiss weakly. Her eyes flickered and glowed but no deadly blast issued.

Her hisses turned to frustrated shrieks as Mads began to walk the length of the bench towards the furnace.

"Now!" Emily screamed.

Mads launched the glittering crystal towards the open maw of the furnace. Juliana raged and thrashed against her bonds but failed as the green shard disappeared inside the fiery depths.

"What have you DONE!" Screamed the ruined upper half of Gabriel. "It will explode." He began scrabbling towards the lower half of his body. He found a chunk and pressed it against his chest. "You've killed us ALL!"

Juliana thrashed with renewed vigour and with a ripping sound, fell from the ceiling. Mads leapt clear as the witch landed on the bench with a bone-crunching thud.

"We've got to go!" Mads yelled. "I see an exit."

The furnace began to roar and spit. Ghostly blasts of golden light sputtered from it, lighting up the whole room briefly.

Emily saw where Mads had pointed and swept her up, pelting for the door.

It burst open and jammed on a pile of rubbish. Metal steps lead up into darkness briefly illuminated by flashes from the furnace.

Emily glanced back into the room to see Gabriel clutching at his lower half. It was beginning to melt and form into a whole. He would be up soon.

Hanging onto the railing for fear of tripping, Emily thundered up the skeletal staircase. The inferno below was gathering; now the ground was shaking. Bits of rust, grit, flakes of concrete rained down and clattered noisily on the metal steps.

One last flight and they were at the top. Emily pushed the release bar but it had jammed. She took a step back and threw herself against it. The door fell open and she ran out into the cold air.

Ahead of her, across the derelict roadway was a grassy bank which she scaled just as the ground lurched.

She threw herself over the edge of the bank and watched as a jet of fire spewed from the door that they had just escaped from.

Flames lit up the squat two story wing above the plant room. It filled with fire as if it were liquid pouring from room to room.

Jets of flame burst from the windows and behind it, the brick chimney gushed incandescent gouts of sparks and smoke high into the air before slowly folding into two and collapsing onto the building beneath it.

It fell in upon itself like a house of cards, sending a writhing inferno twisting into the air lighting up the low clouds above like city lights.

Emily flopped onto her back catching her breath and looking up at the sky. Her cold breath burst into orange puffs as it rose out of the shadows and was caught by the blaze.

Mads crawled up to the top of the bank to watch the building as it continued to burn. From time to time, a piece of wall would give way and crash to the ground.

The dancing flames reflected in her black bead eyes as she stood motionless, staring at the scene of ruin.

In the distance, the sounds of gathering fire engines and police drifted ever closer.

"So." Mads began solemnly, "That's it then?"

"Yeah, she's dead for sure. I reckon the fall probably finished her, what do you think?"

"No, I mean that was our only chance to get my body back."

Emily sat up and looked at Mads sadly. "Honestly, I don't think there was ever a chance." The firelight caught a tear rolling down her grubby face. "Not since I heard him slip up – calling Juliana his mistress, you know, in her house? We've been had."

Mads nodded and turned back to watch the destruction progress. "I didn't know you still carried that practice doll about with you."

"Always." She sniffed, "It was too cute to throw away."

"Nice touch shoving your power bank up its arse."
Mads chuckled.

Emily smiled, "Come on. We'd better get going or we'll have to explain all this to the cops."

The fire was well under way and was now threatening to engulf the main hospital building.

A small heap of burning building slumped, then shifted, heaved upwards a little. A clawed hand pushed aside the glowing bricks and flaming wood as Gabriel heaved himself out from the wreckage.

He padded dejectedly across the car park making hissing sounds as glowing feet scorched the damp moss beneath him.

He sat on the same grassy bank that Mads and Emily had rested on just minutes before and stared back at the flames.

The first of the fire tenders had arrived and the crew were busily hefting the wire mesh panels to one side.

He had cooled now to a dull red, but hot enough to cause the damp grass underneath him to blacken and burn.

What to do now? He sighed and rubbed his chin.

"Maledicta in vita mea," he mumbled. His chin was bare. "That took me a decade to grow."

He got up slowly and ambled away into the night, making little popping noises as he cooled.

CHAPTER 14

IT WAS STILL cold, but at least the evening was dry.

Emily trudged back across the estate, bulging shopping bag handles cutting into each hand. They had fixed the street light near the bins at last; replaced it with one of those new LED ones which let you actually see proper colours at night rather than just muddy orange.

There was a sound from behind the big blue dumpster and a pointed snout peeped out to sniff the air. Emily stopped to watch as a slender fox emerged then paused, looking directly at her. Was it the same one she had seen earlier, at the old hospital? She crouched down and offered her hand outstretched to sniff – but tensed to pull away in case it got nippy.

It trotted over confidently and sniffed her hand, even gave it a little lick.

"You again?" Emily smiled and giggled; such a friendly animal. She stepped over to the curb and sat cross-legged. The fox followed and nonchalantly climbed up into her lap and curled up.

This was wonderful! The little fox was so warm and soft, she couldn't resist the urge to gently stroke it from head all the way round to its bushy orange tail which it had curled around under its chin.

"You'll get fleas in that big merkin of yours." Came a sudden, but familiar voice from behind her.

Immediately, the hair on the back of the fox's neck bristled and it showed its white, needle-like teeth in the direction of Gabriel who had stepped out into the road in front of them.

Emily soothed and shushed the fox, stroking it firmly at its neck. It settled a little, but she could still feel the tension in its body, fixing the gargoyle with a wary glare.

"Why aren't I surprised you're still alive?" Emily intoned.

He crouched, wrapping his slender tail around in front of him, the arrowhead tip bobbing like an aggravated cat tail.

"Not for long. Running on fumes now, I think they say."

"Well, don't think you can come crawling back to me. I don't want anything to do with you." She paused, remembering what he had just said. "Merkin!?" She shouted, suddenly figuring out what those mysterious splashes of sand in the bathroom were. "Have you been perving on me in the shower? You have, haven't you, you lecherous freak!"

There was a bottle in the gutter which she picked up and hefted at the disgusting imp. It hit him squarely in the neck and shattered. "Fuck off and never come back!" She yelled.

Gabriel brandished a clawed middle finger and scampered away cackling into the night.

Shaking her head, Emily thrust her head into the soft fur of the fox and let out a shuddering sigh.

So soft.

She could feel the tension leaving her – and there was that strangely familiar smell again. Not at all what you'd expect from a wild animal, almost like some kind of tropical shampoo smell?

The fox stretched luxuriously and stepped out of Emily's lap. "We need to talk."

Emily jumped and tipped over backwards then scrambled to her knees to stare at the fox... The FOX that had just spoken to her.

"We– We what? But," she spluttered. She looked left and right, but there was nobody about in the parking area – just her under the streetlamp... and a talking fox.

"Don't you recognise me?" it asked, sitting primly.

Emily squinted, "I. I saw a fox at the hospital, and there's been one that I guess looks like you hanging about here. I dunno, I guess all foxes look the same to me?"

"It's me, Kelley. Kelley Stranack," she revealed, tilting her head.

Emily put her hand to her mouth to stifle a cry of

surprise. "Oh, shit! It *is* you! Yes, the red hair, the ponytail... *The coconut shampoo!* Oh my God." She sat back down on the curb, legs crossed but continued to stare at the fox – Kelley – sitting opposite her.

"Would it be stupid of me to ask *how*?" Emily asked.

"You've read about shapeshifters?" she asked simply.

"Oh wow." Emily breathed, "Like in books and stuff. It's all true?"

"Some of it, yes."

"Can you change when you like, or is it like some kind of werewolf thing?"

"Any time." If it were possible for a fox to have a smug expression, then Kelley's face was the epitome of foxy self-satisfaction, "But not right now. It's bloody freezing and clothes don't shift."

Emily giggled, "Your fur is lovely and warm."

Kelley walked over and leaned against her; Emily buried her face in her thick orange fur. "That's nice," came the muffled response.

"There's someone you need to meet." Suddenly all business-like.

"Who?" Emily was grinning from ear to ear, then all at once her face straightened. She sat up and looked at Kelley.

"Um, that warm and fuzzy feeling; that's something else I do." She turned to sit opposite again. "You need to go see my boss. Something important is going to happen and I need you to bring Mads along too."

Emily cleared her throat, the mood really had suddenly changed, but she was all ears. "When? What's it about? Are we in trouble?"

"Tomorrow morning, we'll send a car at ten. I can't really talk about it right now but no, you're not in any kind of trouble."

"Thank goodness," Emily breathed, "I've been expecting the police to come knocking about burning the old hospital down." She stopped to reflect for a moment. "Okay, we'll come. Who's your boss? Dr Franklin?"

Kelley stood and turned to leave. "You don't need to worry about the police," she said over her shoulder, her huge tail waving gently from side to side. "You'll like my boss," she added running off. "His name's Marcus." Came the cry from the distance.

The car, when it arrived attracted more than a little attention. You don't get too many limousines in the run-down tower blocks.

Emily looked up to see who was wolf-whistling from the walkways as she approached the car, but whoever it was ducked out of sight when the driver got out.

The two teens who were admiring the hub caps scattered when they clocked the ape of a man that emerged from the driver's seat. Whoever had sent him couldn't have picked a better character to ward off the locals; bald head, dark glasses, black suit – gigantic.

He opened the passenger door and gestured to Emily to get in. The window glass looked about an inch thick. Were they out to impress or protect her, she wondered.

"Thanks," she attempted, but it just came out as a

squeak.

The door thumped closed and all of a sudden, the outside world was as if it were a million miles away behind the soundproof – and probably bullet-proof – glass.

Instinctively, she buckled up and immediately, the huge car pushed away, silent as a ghost – electric?

"Good morning ma'am." The driver's voice over the speaker was surprisingly gentle. Emily peered through the separating glass to see if there was someone else up front.

"Er, hi." She didn't really know what else to say.

"The journey should be a little over two hours today," he explained. "Traffic leaving the city is light, so we should be on time. Please help yourself to drinks and snacks from the mini-bar."

Emily's eyebrows shot up, 'mini bar?'

Then as if reading her mind, "Sorry, no alcoholic drinks stocked today." He paused and glanced up in the rear-view mirror. "Perhaps the other young lady might like to make herself more comfortable too?"

"Me?" Mads had kept herself quiet, dangling inertly on her keychain up until now.

"Good morning to you too miss."

"Well, this *is* fancy!" Mads unclipped herself and hopped into Emily's lap.

"Thank you," the driver replied, "If either of you need anything please just press the communication button." And with that, the glass snapped to opaque.

By the time the car had begun to make its way up a long, straight driveway to what turned out to be a vast mansion house, Emily had 'fully enjoyed' the complementary snacks and drinks – two *sharing* bags of crisps, chocolate bar, a tin of coke, something fizzy and mango flavoured... and now she needed to pee, badly.

A little embarrassed at how much she had eaten, she shoved the trash into her rucksack.

As the car pulled up to the entrance, the glass turned clear again.

"I hope you both had an enjoyable journey. Miss Madeline, please be at liberty to move freely about the facility. The others are expecting you." He stepped out of the car and held the door open for them. "Miss Emily, if you wish to freshen up before your appointment, Miss Stranack will show you to the powder room."

"Kelley's here?" Emily looked to the grand entrance of the building.

"Mr Felton felt that a familiar face would be comforting."

Mads looked at Emily for a moment before she jumped excitedly down from the car and ran across the gravel to the gigantic steps. Emily climbed out and looked up in awe at the vast stately home.

"Oh, one second..." The driver leaned into the back of the car, then handed Emily an exotic looking chocolate bar with foreign writing on it, "I know you'd wanted to try this one," he added conspiratorially, "One of my favourites."

How did he know?

"Em! Look!" Mads cried from the top of the stone steps.

Emily looked up to see Kelley standing in the huge doorway. She trotted down the steps as Mads capered happily around her ankles. She dashed forward and threw her arms around her.

"Oh, Kelley it's so good to see you again... In person that is."

Kelley laughed and stepped back, "Emily, Madeline. There's some good news." She tried to put on a serious face, but the smile in her eyes was irrepressible.

Emily tilted her head, askance.

"Just come inside, meet Marcus. He'll explain."

"Whatever it is, can it wait a minute? I *have* to pee!"

Mads craned her neck inside the gigantic entrance hall while Emily paid the price of raiding the snack bar.

"You're not going to give any clues?" Mads asked.

"Honestly, this one's for the boss. It's kind of complicated."

Emily emerged, looking a lot more relaxed. "Okay then!" She said cheerfully.

Kelley led them off to a large and cosy room which Emily guessed from playing Cluedo and watching episodes of Agatha Christie mysteries was the library.

A man unfolded from a wing-backed chair as they entered, dropping a cigarette into an ornate ashtray at his side.

"Ah, ladies." He strode across the room, arm outstretched to shake Emily firmly by the hand. He was a thin, stick-insect of a man but his grip was alarmingly strong.

He knelt down to look at Mads, who stood to the side of Emily. "Utterly charmed to meet you." He didn't offer a hand, but stood up and motioned them to sit.

"Just glad to be back with people again," Mads said, climbing up onto the arm of the chair which Emily had claimed.

Marcus sat and nodded quietly. He scratched idly at his neatly trimmed goatee as if he were deciding something.

"Okay." He said suddenly. It made Emily jump. "Here's the thing. We can get your Madeline here back into her old body – fix her up, good as new."

There. It was said.

Emily sat for a second or two, literally slack jawed and speechless. Did he just say...?

"But." She began, she realised that her heart was racing, Mads was gripping her thumb in both of her mitten-hands, she looked up.

"But how?" Mads stepped in, "I'm dead, my body's on a slab, they're having some kind of funeral thing in a couple of days."

"No," Marcus began slowly. He seemed a little ill at ease. "We have it downstairs. It's being prepared."

"But we've already talked about this. Gabriel said he could magic up a body for Mads, but if she's dead, and then just turns up doesn't that make things... tricky?"

"Yes, it would." Marcus leaned back in his chair, "But, well, you know administrative errors in busy hospitals can happen."

A grin started to spread across Emily's face. There was a lot more going on here than she had imagined.

"It's not too much to alter some paperwork here,

a computer record there–" he looked over at Kelley, "Swap out a body."

"What exactly is this place?" Emily blurted out, "You're Kelley's boss, is this some kind of experimental clinic or something shady?"

Marcus smiled, "No, it's nothing like that at all." He chuckled, "Nothing at all. This is just one of our many... facilities. I run an organisation that's, well let's just say it's set up to look after people like yourselves from time to time." He picked up his cigarette and took a long draw, blowing the smoke quickly up into the air above him. "Kelley is one of my best, and most talented operatives. She's been looking out for you, making sure the hospital follows the plot."

"You know she can turn into a fox don't you?" Emily said, instantly realising how stupid that sounded.

"Oh yes, she's very good. She's also an excellent empathic. How do you think she managed to infiltrate the hospital?"

Emily thought for a moment, how she had always felt so at ease around her.

"But to the business at hand." Marcus continued. "Madeline, you do want to be restored to your former body don't you?"

"Hell yeah!"

"Very good then. Kelley, would you send for Bernard?"

Emily whipped her head around. She'd forgotten she had been standing by the door. She nodded silently and slipped out of the room.

"Bernard will be carrying out the procedure today. He's something of an expert in his field. Trained by the best there ever was."

"You don't have the top man on the job then?" Mads quipped.

"Sadly, no. His mentor met with... an unfortunate accident just last year."

"Will it hurt her?" Emily asked, "What are the risks?"

I think that's best left for Bernard to answer. Ah." His face fell, briefly at the sound of a small dog approaching from outside, "Here he comes now. And that... dog."

The yapping grew louder until a slightly mangy looking pug barrelled into the room, collided with the side of a sofa and sat stupidly shaking its head.

"Um, Ladies, can I introduce you to Fou-Fou. She belonged to our late operative."

"Oh, she's sweet." Emily reached out to stroke her. Fou-Fou looked up to her, eyes pointing in slightly odd directions. When Emily pulled her hand away, it was covered in fur that had come away in clumps.

"Oh," she brushed the hair off on her jeans, "Is she very old?"

"About fifty." Came a haughty voice from the door. "From what I hear."

"In dog years? That's not so bad." Emily said, eyeing the dog warily as it slowly toppled onto its back, panting hoarsely.

"Actual years. Good afternoon, you must be Emily. Bernard Denby, necromancer in chief." He held out a bony hand. Behind her, Marcus grimaced.

Emily took the proffered hand and shook it gingerly, it was cold. She knew what a necromancer was from books and films, and his appearance didn't disappoint – thin, and with all the charm of a Victorian undertaker.

"Woah, cool. You're an *actual* necromancer?" Emily was impressed. Denby nodded slowly, the shadow of a smirk on his thin, bloodless lips.

Mads climbed up onto the back of the chair to get a better look, "So, what, you're going to bring me back as a zombie? I'm not so sure about that."

He turned curtly and nodded at Mads, "A zombie, no. Let me explain if you will permit. It is possible, with the application of the appropriate rites, infusions and essential life forces to re-animate the body of one who has passed."

Both girls nodded, rapt. Marcus sucked his teeth and continued smoking his cigarette.

"But the body which then lives and breathes is but an empty vessel, a puppet or dumb servant."

"Like Juliana's two goons," Mads put in excitedly.

"Indeed. And the delightful Fou-Fou here also."

Marcus choked briefly, and Emily was sure he swore. Denby's eyes flicked briefly to Marcus and back, his expression unchanging, "Yours is an exceedingly rare case, where the life force and very essence of your being is still intact."

"But the body," Emily began, her voice wavering, "The burns, her heart?"

"Oh, that? Easily fixed." Denby waved his fingers dramatically, "All good as new. Pumping regular as a Swiss watch."

"Pumping?" Mads asked warily.

"Yes, of course. The body is all prepared for you now. As soon as you are ready, we can begin. It's warmed up and, well ticking over you might say." He looked pleased with himself.

"We're *cheating death?*" Mads' voice was full of awe and fear in equal measure. "That never ends well."

"You never really *died* as such," The necromancer said nonchalantly, "Not a case of cheating, more a sleight of hand."

Emily's mouth hung open, this was all happening so fast. "Mads, shit." She turned and picked her up, "You're coming back."

"I'm not sure what I was expecting." Emily said, looking around the room.

In the centre, on what looked like a hospital operating table, lay Mads' body covered up to the shoulders in a green sheet. Medical monitors traced vital statistics, drip bags of some kind of pale yellow solution hung from a stand, their tubes snaking under the sheet.

She put her hand to her mouth when she noticed Mads— *Mads' body's* chest gently rising and falling.

Mads was clinging onto Emily's shoulder and could see the whole scene for herself.

"Christ, Em. This is the freakiest thing I've ever seen. It's *me* there."

"Quite something, isn't it?" Bernard said reverently. "The human body. Like this–" He gestured towards the table, "The most intricate machine in the known universe. But add just that one extra spark." He turned and looked to Mads and Emily, "Something *infinitely* more."

"So, what now?" Mads asked.

Bernard nodded slowly. "Next, we release your consciousness from this temporary vessel and guide it back to where it truly belongs.

"The body is ready. It functions well, I repaired the issue with the heart and I have been feeding it for two days. It needs to heal a little after being dormant – expunge toxins, regenerate damaged tissue."

"What's in the drip?" Emily asked, pointing to the two large bags.

"My own concoction. It's mostly what the doctors would call Hartman's Solution, fluids, glucose, salts plus a sedative, antibiotics and a few rather special elements that perhaps established medicine might not necessarily approve of – but it's safe, I assure you."

Mads gazed down at her body, the lights over the operating table glinting in her black eyes.

Someone pushed a trolley into the room. It was covered with a blue cloth and contained one item – a metal tray just large enough for Mads to lie down in.

"This is it then?" Mads asked, nervously, "Will it hurt?"

"At first, no. Your consciousness doesn't feel pain in the way that the body does; but I'm sorry, there will be pain. Once you connect with your flesh and blood body, you will feel it again as you used to. Take that as a good sign. You'll know you're home. But the body still has some healing to do. The painkillers we've introduced should help at first, and you can take more afterwards."

"Oh, God Mads. Are you sure you want to do this?"

She turned and pushed herself against Emily's face, she still had a faint aroma of coffee, "Of course. It'll be worth it." She leapt from Emily's shoulder and landed soundlessly on the trolley. "Let's go."

"So be it. Madeline, if you would." He indicated the metal tray. "It's not elegant, but I do need you to stay more or less still so that I can focus the energies."

Mads lay in the tray and folded her arms across her chest. Bernard turned and busied himself on the other side of the operating table.

"As this is a very delicate process, it is absolutely vital that I am not disturbed in any way once I have begun. I would ask everyone to move to the viewing gallery and remain there until summoned." He indicated another door that Emily hadn't noticed next to a large glass window, blackness beyond.

"Come on, I'll show you." Kelley placed her hand on Emily's arm and led her through the door. Marcus followed with a severe look on his face.

Inside, were a row of ornately carved wooden chairs padded with red velvet.

"These look more the part for occult rituals," she muttered to herself as she sat.

"He's a bit of a ponce, that Bernard." Marcus scoffed, "He'd have that bleedin' operating theatre done up in wood panels if he had his own way."

Emily turned to give him an odd look but he just smiled back. Warmly, this time.

Bernard had donned a heavy scarlet robe and was now pacing slowly around the room wafting smoke from something in a wooden bowl.

To her side, Marcus shook his head slowly.

"I get the impression you don't like Bernard," Emily said quietly.

"Oh, it's not *him* per se. It's *his lot*." He'd dropped the posh accent completely now.

"No, I've never really seen eye to eye with necromancers. Oh, we *need* them from time to time but... well. They give me the creeps."

Emily giggled involuntarily.

"But old Bernard's just about the best there is. Mads is in good hands. Ah, look he's done fucking about with the burning sage."

Bernard was now standing dramatically at the head of the operating table, his velvet hood covering his face.

It had begun.

At first, there was nothing obvious to see, then a faint golden cloud began to form over Mads in the shiny tray. Soon, tiny sparks and twinkles could be seen in the cloud, like miniscule specks of dust catching the sunlight.

Over the course of a minute or two, the cloud grew in density and size, the twinkles becoming brighter. Within the cloud could, tendrils turning and twisting over and over, slowly changing and folding forever in on themselves.

It's working. Mads thought to herself. *I'm out, I can see the whole room.*

Floating in the air above her old cloth body, Mads felt the most intense sensation of pure *freedom* she had ever known. She could feel the space she was in as if pure dimension itself was the most luxurious carpet she was sprawled upon. She stretched out to feel more and it was bliss.

But now there was pressure. It constrained her, it

made her... small. No, this was wrong, she wanted to touch the very edges of the universe.

"She's losing density." Bernard grunted, the effort to contain Mads into a finite volume was making his outstretched hands tremble. Perspiration beaded his brow, unseen beneath the cowl. "Come on, don't fight it."

"What does he mean?" Emily gasped, rising from her chair and peering through the glass, "What's happening?"

"Don't worry," Kelley said softly, "It's under control. He just needs to make sure she doesn't... I'm not sure how to put it into words, well kind of evaporate?"

"What? No!" Emily cried. Putting her palms against the glass, "Don't let her die!"

Bernard yelled with the effort, a light blue glow began to form around his hands and lower arms.

At last, the cloud that had now filled most of the room began to collapse in on itself, slowly at first, but then rushing in, with streaks of gold into a dazzling and furious ball of twisting, spinning energy no larger than a fist.

Screaming incantations, Bernard clutched his fists together and the ball of life slowly drifted towards the comatose body. It hovered a hand's breadth above the forehead, then in a blink, the golden light sucked itself in through the eyes, ears, nose, mouth.

And abruptly it was gone.

Marcus drew his breath in slowly and deliberately but said nothing.

Emily pulled her hands away from the glass, leaving a

pair of palm prints outlined faintly with condensation. She turned to Marcus, slightly breathless.

"What happened? Did it work?"

"I... Don't know," he said, not breaking eye contact with Bernard, who was still standing motionless at the head of the table.

"Kelley," imploring now, "Is she alive?"

There was no answer. She began pounding on the thick glass, yelling, "Tell me! What happened?"

Kelley quietly got to her feet and put her arms around Emily from behind, engulfing her in warmth and calmness.

"No. No, don't." Emily struggled free, feeling the icy cold of fear flood back through her.

In the operating theatre, Bernard slowly drew his hood back. He turned to look towards the window and silently beckoned them inside.

Emily bolted to the gallery door and across the room. Her eyes caught the metal dish in which the cloth doll lay inert and utterly lifeless.

"Mads!" she cried, falling on the body on the table, holding her pale face in her hands. She ran her fingers along the birthmark line from her jaw to her hairline. Her skin felt warm, soft, ALIVE.

Abruptly, her eyelids flickered. Emily jumped, startled.

Again, a slight flicker. Emily brought her face in close.

Slowly, Madeline's eyes opened, blinked and focussed on Emily's face, hovering above, eyes brimming with tears.

"Hulluh..." she mumbled.

Emily beamed, stifled a sob.

"Hulluh... Llll... chhhkn," she attempted again, groggy with sedative. But very much alive.

Emily dissolved into joyous sobs of happiness, burying her head into her neck and holding her tightly as if she might simply cease to exist.

THE END

EPILOGUE

THE FLAKING BLUE paint above the little shop had seen better days, but the name 'Crystal Energy' was still bright and clear, even in the half-moonlight.

Gabriel raised himself stiffly up to peer through the grubby windows. The shop itself was in darkness, but in the back room, the lights were on and somebody was still moving about.

With a painful grinding sound, the gargoyle limped to the glass door set back from the street and pressed his face against the glass. He scratched pitifully at the window.

He was dying.

This was his last hope.

The man in the shop stopped at the shrill claw

against glass, sighed and put his mug down.

Bamboo chimes rattled as the door opened and Marcus peered down at the pitiful creature on his doorstep.

"Jesus wept!" he sighed, "Get inside, look at the state of you. You're a mess."

It was true. His ability to regenerate and hold his shape was beginning to fail as his energy depleted. Where he once looked freshly carved, he now resembled his original brethren still adorning an ancient church not too far from here.

He looked weathered.

"I know what you want," Marcus growled as Gabriel hobbled inside.

He looked up expectantly, "To come around full circle, *home* with my first and true master."

Marcus span around, "NO!" He spat, "I'll never take you back into service."

"But you first carved me, with your own hands. You remember?"

"Yes, I remember. I also remember what a treacherous little *shit* you are!"

Gabriel cowered, trying his best to put on a pathetic show for sympathy but it was wasted.

"I'll never, ever forget nor *forgive* you for what you did, the company you fell in with when I needed you most. And now, you hang about with a common street witch like some mangy cat."

"But she's gone now, I—"

"I fucking know she's gone. I saw to it."

A sour and crafty look washed across the gargoyle's battered face. "I'll expose you," he said slowly, his

234

options were evaporating fast. "I'll show myself, tell everyone who and *what* you are. You'll be finished." His voice changed, saccharine sweet, "But if you take me back, I could never do that – I'd be bound." He held out his hand, grinning.

"Enough." Marcus turned and stalked towards the back room. There was a heavy thump behind him.

Shortly, he returned with his mug of tea and cigarette, which was burning low.

With a grim face, he surveyed the inert stone figure in the middle of his shop floor – weather-beaten, ugly as sin with one outstretched hand.

He stubbed out the dog-end into the palm and vanished behind the heavy curtains at the back of the old shop.

Thanks for reading!
We hope you enjoyed this book.
If you did then please consider leaving a review or a rating at Amazon – it would mean a lot to us all.

MORE FROM
sci-fi-cafe

Available to buy in paperback and eBook from
Amazon and other good online stores.
Scan the affiliate links in the QR codes to find out
more about each book.

Look out for our Audiobooks on
Audible and Amazon too

Transplant
Greenways
The Tribe
The Seed Garden

Our Paranormal and Paranormal Romance books
are all set in the same world and can be read in any
order or separately.

The Threads Which Bind us
The Wolf Inside us
Into Dust
The Calico Golem

The Threads Which Bind us

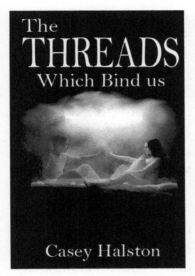

Anna's life is falling apart. She's skipping college, lost touch with her friends and can't face her family. She wakes late to find the ghost of a young man in her room. He has no memory of his past life nor any clue as to why he has appeared here.

In the beginning, she fights to get rid of him, but something about his glasslike sensuality fascinates her as he is drawn towards the only person in his world that can hear him, see him, *touch* him.

As they work to find out who he is, how he died and what is keeping him in the realm of the living, Anna's own recent and tragic past surfaces.

Content advisory: Mild sex references, suicide references. Alcohol.

ISBN: 978-1-910779-98-9

The Wolf Inside Us

Jake is a reclusive genius shut away in his penthouse apartment where he draws his award winning zombie comics. Kat is one of his biggest fans. She's also his publisher's office manager and each week gets to visit Jake to see his latest work.

Over the years, Kat has developed a soft spot for Jake, so it's not surprising that she's completely thrown when he suddenly disappears. But stranger still, why did he leave a tiny puppy behind, all alone, and where did he get it?

Kat's relationship grows from more than simple puppy love in this sensual werewolf romance where life throws all it has at this girl and her dog.

Content advisory: Mild sex and fantasy sex references, alcohol, mild fantasy violence.

ISBN 978-1-910779-97-2

Into Dust

Ryan Malin had made a name for himself as the author of a very successful series of guidebooks on supposedly haunted houses. But there was always one that had been off-limits to him - Hewitson Cottage.

That was until he was approached by the alluring Kelley Stranack. She and her fellow university lecturer promised a whole weekend of exclusive access, all expenses paid. Naturally, he jumped at the chance.

Of course none of the places he'd written about were actually haunted, but this place... well, it had a history worth investigating.

But why had a cash-strapped university chosen HIM, paid all his expenses and who had paid for the cottage to be refurbished for their trip?

ISBN 978-1-910779-05-7

The Girl from the Temple Ruins

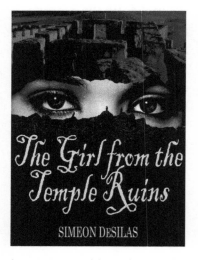

A temple to the goddess Amalishah lies in the remotest wastelands of Assyria. She is their protector but to others she is known as The Monster. The Hittite prince Artaxias visits the Palace of the Goddess to implore the temple priests to free prisoners captured from the border. He knows their fate, the appalling human sacrifice that will be made to the goddess who must feed on human blood.

Four thousand years have eroded the memory and the evidence of these events until British archaeologist Michael Townsend discovers the subterranean lair of the goddess. Michael is visited and instantly captivated by a mysterious and beautiful woman. The Hittites called her monster, a creature now called vampire.

ISBN: 978-1910779-41-5

City of Storms

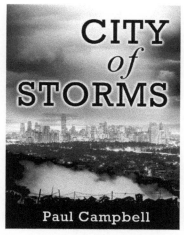

When top foreign correspondent Sean Brian flies into Manila in the Philippines, a typhoon and a political revolution are uppermost in his thoughts.

But what also awaits will turn his already busy life into a roller coaster of romance, adventure, elation and despair.

At the centre of this transformation is an infant boy child, born, abandoned and plunged into street poverty in the grim underbelly of an Asian metropolis.

This is the catalyst for a story ranging from the corrupt, violent world of back street city sex clubs and drug addiction, to the clean air of the Sulu Sea and the South Pacific; from the calm safety of an island paradise to the violent guerilla world of the notorious Golden Triangle and the southern Philippines archipelago.

As we follow the child, Bagyo, into fledgling manhood, we can only wonder at the ripples that spread from one individual to engulf so many others – and at the injustice that still corrodes life on the mean streets of the world.

ISBN: 978-1908387-99-8

Milton Keynes UK
Ingram Content Group UK Ltd.
UKHW010711230624
444490UK00001B/71